D1375087

00490919 3

one hundred and forty-eight countries. Of course, he travelled at a time when the aeroplane was just being invented, when people communicated by letter or telegraph, and so he travelled by motor car, ship, horse, and even by elephant and camel – there were few places on Earth that he wouldn't visit. He had many wonderful adventures, some of which may very well be in the story that you are about to read . . .

We are so pleased that you are about to embark on an adventure with the wise Hal and the impulsive Roger, and we wish you luck as you search with them for unusual wildlife and great adventure.

The granddaughters of Willard Price:

Katharine Price
Susannah Price Haney
Rebecca Price Brooks

WILLARD PRICE

GORILLA ADVENTURE

Illustrated from drawings by Pat Marriott

RED FOX

GORILLA ADVENTURE
A RED FOX BOOK 978 1 849 41748 8

First published in Great Britain by Jonathan Cape Ltd
An imprint of Random House Children's Publishers UK
A Random House Group Company

Jonathan Cape edition published 1969
Red Fox edition published 1993
This edition published 2012

1 3 5 7 9 10 8 6 4 2

The Random House Group Limited supports the Forest Stewardship Council
(FSC), the leading international forest certification organization. Our books
carrying the FSC label are printed on FSC -certified paper. FSC is the only
forest certification scheme endorsed by the leading environmental
organizations, including Greenpeace. Our paper procurement policy can be
found at www.randomhouse.co.uk/environment.

Red Fox Books are published by Random House Publishers UK,
61–63 Uxbridge Road, London W5 5SA

www.randomhousechildrens.co.uk
www.totallyrandombooks.co.uk
www.randomhouse.co.uk

Addresses for companies within The Random House Group Limited can be
found at: www.randomhouse.co.uk/offices.htm

THE RANDOM HOUSE GROUP Limited Reg. No. 954009

A CIP catalogue record for this book is available from the British Library.

Printed in the UK by CPI Group (UK) Ltd, Croydon, CR0 4YY

GORILLA
ADVENTURE

By the same author:

Amazon Adventure
South Sea Adventure
Arctic Adventure
Safari Adventure
Elephant Adventure
Underwater Adventure
Lion Adventure
Whale Adventure
Tiger Adventure
African Adventure
Diving Adventure
Cannibal Adventure
Volcano Adventure

GORILLA ADVENTURE

Contents

1
Congo Jungle

Hal and Roger had grown up with animals. Their earliest memories were of wild beasts.

For all of Hal's nineteen years and his brother's fourteen, their daily companions had been kangaroos, giraffes, elephants, rhinos, hippos, lions, leopards and a hundred other creatures great and small that roamed the animal farm of their father, John Hunt, famous animal collector.

The farm was on Long Island, New York. There the animals were kept until they could be sold to zoos or circuses.

The boys had accompanied their father on several expeditions to such faraway places as the Amazon jungle, the South Seas and the heart of Africa. They had learned the dangerous art of taking wild animals alive. Now John Hunt was getting a bit old for so rough a life, therefore the boys were going it alone.

They had just completed a job in the African lion country. A cable from their father gave them a new project.

RINGLING CIRCUS WANTS GIANT GORILLA, BIG CHIMPS, PYTHON, GABOON VIPER, SPITTING COBRA, AND OTHER TYPICAL WILDLIFE FOR JUNGLE EXHIBIT. WHAT CAN YOU DO?

It was a thrilling and challenging assignment. Hal talked it over with Joro, chief of his thirty-man African crew. Joro shook his head.

'Very difficult,' he said. 'Those are bad snakes. And there's only one place to find that giant gorilla.'

'Where is that?'

'Congo jungle. Between Congo River and Virunga volcanoes. Wild country and wild people. Tribes fight, men die. Perhaps you tell your father no.'

But the boys were not in the habit of saying no when their father asked them to do a job, especially when it was one that offered excitement, adventure, and a chance to learn more about Africa and its wildlife.

So their reply was an enthusiastic yes.

Their enthusiasm simmered down a bit when they crossed from the lion country into the jungle home of the gorillas.

Joro had told the truth. The Congo was not at peace. The government was friendly towards foreigners. But tribes in the back country were killing foreign visitors. And the gorillas had no use for any man, white or black.

The Hunts got their permit from the commandant at Rumangabo.

'The Virunga volcano territory is pretty wild,' the commandant warned them. 'You'll need a guide.'

'Can you recommend one?'

'No, I can't. We did have some good hunters. But when the Congo boiled over, they went back to Belgium. One of them stayed – but I don't recommend him.'

'Why not?' Hal asked. 'If he had enough courage to stay, perhaps he's just the man we need.'

The commandant smiled. 'I'm afraid it wasn't courage that kept him here. He just didn't have the cash to go. He was broke – still is.'

'Then perhaps he'd be willing to take on this job. Doesn't he know the country?'

'More or less.'

'Then what's the matter?'

The commandant pursed his lips. 'I think I've said enough. Suppose I send a boy to fetch him. Then you can judge for yourself.'

A half hour later the big Belgian walked in. The commandant introduced him as Andre Tieg.

Tieg's appearance was rather breathtaking. He stood well over six feet, had a massive chest and brawny arms. A great yellow moustache poured out on both sides of his red face and drooped at the ends, dragged down by its thickness and length. It was a moustache in a thousand. It alone should scare any gorilla out of its wits.

Tieg's mouth was thin-lipped as if it had been cut into his face with a knife. His eyebrows were big and bushy. His yellow hair stood up like the crest of an angry cockatoo.

But the most startling thing about him was the way his eyes behaved. Or, rather, the way his right eye behaved. The other stood stock still. It was glass, electric blue, and its fixed stare was frightening.

A deep scar beneath it running all the way down to the corner of the mouth suggested that the eye and cheek had been gouged by the claw of a leopard. The scar warped the left side of the face into a perpetual sneer.

While one eye stood still, the other was as restless as a mouse on a hot stove. It darted this way and that, as if it had to make up for the stillness of its glass neighbour. It crawled over Hal and Roger from head to toe and seemed to disapprove of everything it saw.

Its colour was a washed-out blue that made it look as blank as the window of an empty house. Altogether the face had a curiously unreal appearance with its ghastly scar and ghostly eyes and slash of a mouth.

Hal put him down as a vain, hard, and perhaps cruel man, not quite the sort of fellow one would feel safe with in the woods.

'Yes, yes,' said Tieg. 'I know the gorilla country. I'll guide you. Of course I'm a very busy man, but I happen to be free at present. But you must understand, the

Congo is in a very troubled state. You shouldn't have come. Most Europeans are going home.'

'But you haven't gone,' Hal said.

Tieg swelled visibly. His high brush of hair nearly touched the ceiling.

'I'm hard to scare. I'm not afraid of the locals. And I'm not afraid of gorillas. But you must not expect too much. There aren't many mountain gorillas left.'

'I realize that,' Hal said.

'You see,' said Tieg importantly with the sort of voice an encyclopaedia would have if it could speak, 'there are two kinds of gorillas – the mountain gorilla and the lowland gorilla. The lowland gorilla lives in the hot, wet jungle along the West Coast. It is short-haired and small-jawed. It's about the same height and weight as the mountain gorilla – but doesn't look it. The mountain gorilla appears almost twice as large, because he's covered with hair eight inches long. That's nature's way of protecting him against the cold. His home is about ten thousand feet up on the slopes of the volcanoes – and it gets really chilly up there, especially at night. The lowland gorilla would die in that climate. Why don't you go after the lowlanders? They're easier to get.'

'I know,' Hal said.

Tieg's glass eye stared coldly. 'Then aren't you pretty foolish to go after the ones that are harder to get?'

'It's just because they're hard to get that people want them,' Hal explained. 'There are two hundred and nineteen lowland gorillas in captivity the world over. But only thirteen mountain gorillas. A zoo or circus won't pay more than five thousand dollars for a lowland gorilla. What they really want is the rare mountain variety and they'll put up ten thousand dollars to get one.'

'Indeed,' Tieg said. His good eye dropped, but his artificial orb continued to stare. 'Well, young man, it's your funeral.'

The next evening they found themselves in a rough cabin ten thousand feet up the slope of Mount Mikeno. It had been a stiff climb – the fourteen Land-Rovers, Powerwagons, catching cars and jeeps belonging to the expedition had needed every ounce of power they could get out of their four-wheel drive.

Now the two boys and Tieg sat about a rough table, sipped tea, and chewed on the dried meat called jerky.

The crew had made themselves a campfire outside near a sheet of water too large to be called a pool and too small to be called a lake. Night had come on and animals were creeping out of the forest to drink.

Roger peered through a small window. 'I see bush pigs and wildebeest and waterbucks and there are two buffaloes. But no gorillas.'

'Gorillas don't drink often,' Hal said. 'Besides, they seldom come so near camp.'

Tieg cocked his movable eye at the raftered roof. 'You'll see them soon enough. I hope you're prepared for a shock. Beginners like you find them the most terrifying animals on earth.'

'Why terrifying?' Hal asked. 'After all, they look pretty much like men.'

'That's just it,' Tieg said. 'They look so much like men that you expect them to act like men. But when one comes at you with a scream that can be heard ten miles away, with his huge hairy chest blown up like a balloon, his face twisted into a horrible glare, his jaws bigger than any man's, open wide enough to take in your head, his six- or seven-foot body looking like ten feet, his five hundred pounds against your hundred and fifty, his enormous arms buried in hair eight inches long, hands as big as footballs slapping his stomach, *pok-pok-pok*, loud as an African drum, and you realize that here is a monster with the strength of ten men – well, it's such a surprise to see a creature that looks like a man behaving as no man could ever behave that the chills run up and down your spine and you are so scared you stand rooted to the spot, or you run like mad.'

'I'd run,' shivered Roger.

'That would be the worst thing you could do. No, you have to stand your ground. He's faster – if you run he'll catch you, and once those arms go around you you'll quit breathing. Your only chance is to stand and face him. Then he may – he just may – stop and think it over. And he may not. If his wives and children are behind him and he's afraid you may hurt them, he'll keep on coming. If you look harmless and carry no gun, he may throw up his arms as if saying "What's the use?" and go grumbling back to his family.'

Hal knitted his brows. 'Did you say carry no gun? Suppose there's real trouble?'

'There'll be more trouble if you carry a gun. If a gorilla comes for you the best thing you can do with a gun is to throw it into the bushes. Remember, you're dealing with an intelligent creature. Gorilla, chimp, elephant, dolphin – the four most intelligent animals on earth. The gorilla knows a gun when he sees one.'

'Then he must have been hunted.'

'Yes – by some famous hunters – and they stayed right here in this cabin – Prince Wilhelm of Sweden, King Albert of Belgium, Theodore Roosevelt, Sir Julian Huxley, Carl Akeley.' Tieg threw back his head as if sniffing a bad smell. 'I'm wasting my breath,' he said. 'These names wouldn't mean a thing to kids your age.'

Hal smiled. He was surprised by this sudden burst of sarcasm. He didn't bother to say that he had been brought up on tales of the great hunters and knew these names very well.

'But I'll tell you about Carl Akeley,' went on Tieg. 'He thought this spot one of the loveliest on earth. He wanted to be buried here, and he was. You'll see his grave tomorrow morning. He collected animals of every sort in this forest and mounted them. If you ever go to the Natural History Museum in New York you'll see them in the Akeley African Hall.'

Roger spoke up. 'They're great. We've seen them dozens of times.'

Tieg looked at Roger so hard his glare seemed to pierce the boy's hide. 'So I suppose you know more about all this than I do. Perhaps you ought to be the guide and teach me.'

I could teach you better manners, Roger thought.

'There's another man more important in a way than all these,' Tieg went on. 'You wouldn't know about him. He settled down here a few years ago and lived among the gorillas for more than a year. He made the first detailed study of the gorilla's habits. His name was Schaller.'

'I've read his books,' Hal said. He opened his pack and drew out George Schaller's *The Year of the Gorilla*. 'It's my gorilla bible.'

'So that makes you an authority, I suppose,' was Tieg's caustic comment.

'Nonsense,' Hal said. 'I know nothing about the mountain gorilla except what I've read. That's one animal my father never had on the farm. Never could get one.'

'And there's no guarantee that you'll be more successful,' Tieg reminded him. 'You could shoot one easily enough. But to take one alive – that's really something.'

2
Footprints

The boys were too excited to sleep soundly. They were out at dawn to look things over.

The evening before when they had arrived it had been too dark to see much. Now they agreed with Akeley – this was one of the loveliest places in the world.

The small meadow was filled with wild flowers. The lakelet was smooth as a mirror. It reflected the great trees that surrounded the clearing like guards protecting a treasure. It reflected also the rump of a rhino which had finished drinking and was wandering back into the forest with two white egrets riding on his back.

In one corner of the meadow was a flat gravestone bearing the words:

CARL AKELEY
NOVEMBER 17, 1926

Through gaps in the trees could be seen the other Virunga mountains, every one of them a volcano. There were eight altogether, six of them sleeping under snow, two very much alive spouting fire and red-hot lava.

The cabin had rough unpainted board walls and a tin roof. It consisted of three large rooms and two sheds – the crew slept in one room and the sheds, the boys shared a room, Andre Tieg had a room to himself.

Everyone was up now – except Tieg. He was having his beauty sleep. Hal talked with the cook. Then he rapped on Tieg's door.

'Breakfast's ready,' he called.

In due time Tieg came out, yawning.

'What's for breakfast?' he inquired sleepily.

'How would you like three per cent of an egg?'

Tieg glared. 'Is that supposed to be funny?'

'Yes,' Hal said. 'Funny and true. The cook tells me he's scrambled an egg.'

'An egg for each man, you mean. Learn to speak precisely, young fellow.'

'I'm being precise,' Hal said. 'We're going to have one egg for breakfast.'

'One egg for thirty-three men?'

'Exactly.'

Tieg looked at Hal with an expression that would turn milk sour.

'You're talking nonsense,' he snarled. 'Anyhow, I want no egg. Just coffee and toast.'

But he changed his mind when the mountain of scrambled egg came on the outdoor picnic table. He still pretended to be indifferent, but he took a large helping.

'One egg indeed,' he said, looking at the luscious yellow mountain. 'It took at least three dozen eggs to make that.'

'No, just one,' Hal said. 'Cook, bring the shell.'

The cook brought the shell. It was unbroken except for holes he had made in the ends so that he could pour out the contents. The shell was as large as the cook's own head.

Tieg flushed angrily. An ostrich egg, of course. He should have guessed. He had been stupid. The men were smiling, but Tieg lacked a sense of humour – he was not amused.

Hal saw that the big fellow's vanity was hurt and tried to make things right.

'You know,' he said, 'you were very smart. You took one look at that pile and said it must have taken three dozen eggs to make it. You hit the nail right on the head. The egg weighed four pounds. That's almost exactly the weight of three dozen large hen eggs. Enough for thirty-three men and three helpings to spare. And because you were so clever, you get what's left.'

He scraped out the remainder on to Tieg's plate.

Tieg's cockatoo hair seemed to stand up more proudly than ever. While one eye stood still, the other swept around the circle of men.

'Well,' he said, 'it's just a matter of experience. When you reach my age, young man, you'll be a lot wiser.'

'I can't wait,' was the retort that came to Hal's lips. But he didn't say it. He saw that he must be careful not to scratch this big fellow's thin skin.

'Suppose we get going,' he said. 'What do you advise, Andre? By the way, may I call you Andre?'

Andre Tieg's eyebrows went up. 'I shall call you Hal. But I think it would be more fitting if you should call me Mr Tieg.'

'Of course, Mr Tieg. What do you say – shall we scout around first before we actually try to capture a gorilla? Just the three of us – and Joro. He's our chief tracker. Too many men might scare the animals. After we locate a family of gorillas, we can go in again with the men and nets and all.'

'As you please,' Tieg said. 'But Joro will hardly be

necessary. I think probably I know the pugmarks of the gorilla better than he does.'

'I'm sure you do. But suppose we let him come, just to protect us in case of trouble. I must confess you scared us pretty badly when you told us how fierce these beasts can be.'

Tieg smiled indulgently. 'Don't worry,' he said. 'I'll be with you. But your tracker may come, provided he keeps quiet and doesn't get in the way.'

They plunged into the woods. It was not easy going. The forest was not open like a park. The undergrowth was thick and consisted largely of nettles and thistles six feet high. They slapped across one's face, leaving red welts. The thorns of wild blackberry bushes tore at their clothes. Their feet sank in moss so deep that it was hard to pull them out again.

Tieg led the way. He had said he knew this country. For an hour they pushed and scrambled and scratched. Tieg stopped.

'We must be a good three miles from the camp now. Perhaps we'll begin to see gorillas – they like the wild spots. There's an open space ahead. We may find them there.'

They came out into the clearing. It was the one they

had left an hour before. There was the cabin and the little lake and the men, surprised to see them back so soon. Tieg had made a complete circle.

Tieg did his noble best to think of an excuse for this blunder.

'No sun,' he said. 'You can't keep a straight course through the woods if there's no sun.'

His companions began to realize that if they were to find gorillas they must do it without Tieg's help.

Hal went to his pack and pulled out a pocket compass. 'Now we'll know our directions at least,' he said.

Roger was tired. 'All that slogging through moss and thorns for nothing! Aren't there any trails through these woods?'

'No trails,' Tieg said.

'But all the animals that come to this waterhole every night. Surely they must make a path.'

'No path,' Tieg insisted. 'Animals don't need paths.'

Roger was not convinced. He wandered away from the group. He walked along the edge of the meadow, peering into the bushes, parting them here and there to make sure that they did not hide a trail. Fumbling among a shower of yellow hagenia blossoms, he startled an impala gazelle. It did not run away, but leaped soaring twenty feet before it touched ground. In a case like this, Tieg was right. The gazelle did not need a path, and did not make one.

But how about buffaloes, elephants, rhinos and such – heavy beasts that plodded along with all four feet pressing the ground? They wouldn't soar over bushes. They would plough through them or around them, and those that came after would follow those that had gone before, and the result would be a trail. But the thick shrubbery that grew up along the forest's edge might hide the entrance to the trail.

So he kept pushing aside the curtain of foliage, the young tree ferns, the bamboo, the strange wild celery six feet high, the blackberry bushes.

And at last, there it was. Concealed behind the fast-growing screen was the beginning of a path, deeply stamped with the sharp hooves of buffalo, the broad pads of elephants, and many other imprints unfamiliar to Roger.

'I found a trail,' he shouted, and the others came to join the young explorer.

'Good for you,' Hal said, and Joro gave him a smile that was all the more brilliant because of the gleam of very white teeth in a very black face.

Only Tieg was not pleased, and followed sulkily as they struck off along the trail.

To Joro, the trail was a book. It told him what animals had passed this way. 'Warthog,' he said. 'Waterbuck. Kongoni. Topi. Buffalo. Bush pig.' He stopped and looked about. 'Watch both sides – and above. A leopard has been here within the last half hour.'

They went on, warily, until Joro said, 'You can take it easy now. No more leopard prints. Only hyenas and jackals.'

He stopped again and bent down to study the ground. Tieg came up beside him and looked at what he had found.

'No animal made that,' Tieg said. 'One of your men must have wandered across the trail here.'

It did look like a human footprint. At one end of the print, the stamp of five toes was plainly visible.

'But,' Hal said, 'look at the big toe. Far away from the other four. It sticks out to the side, all alone. No man's foot is shaped that way.'

'You don't understand,' said Tieg. 'Feet that have never worn shoes spread out.'

Roger's sharp eyes had found something else. 'Joro,' he said, 'how does a gorilla walk?'

'Well, he can stand up like a man. But he generally walks along on all fours. His feet are pretty flat on the ground. But his hands are not. He keeps his hands doubled up into fists. He walks on his knuckles. The thumb is not used so all you see is the print of four knuckles.'

'Like these?' Roger said, pointing out a row of four deep dents in the ground.

'That's it,' cried Joro, much excited. 'That's it.' He looked about him to make sure that the great ape was not hiding in the bushes. Then he looked back at the print. 'He must be a big fellow.' He pressed his own knuckles into the ground. His row of dents was three inches long. The other print stretched a good six inches.

'Boy!' exclaimed Roger. 'He must have hands like hams. I'd hate to be swatted by one of those.'

3
Gog, the Giant

Joro was carefully examining the ground. 'He went on up this path,' he said. 'Let's follow him. But be very quiet. These prints are fresh – he can't be very far away.'

They went on, careful not to step on any twig that might crack underfoot. After about a quarter of a mile, Joro stopped.

'He left the trail here,' Joro whispered. He stood still and listened. He evidently heard something. The boys heard it too – a sound like the dripping of water from leaves after a storm. But there had been no storm. The bushes were dry. The sound might come from a brook running over stones. No, it couldn't be that, because it wasn't continuous. It came and went, began and stopped.

Then there was another sound – a voice – a deep, contented muttering as of a man talking to himself.

Joro signalled the others to come on, and as silently as a ghost he left the trail and followed the footprints through the bushes. Whenever the voice stopped, he stopped. He stood like a statue until he heard the muttering again or the tinkle of water.

Now they must be very close to the source of these curious sounds. Joro raised his hand. They halted and peered through the bushes.

Little light came down through the trees. In the half-dark they caught the glint of water. There was a small brook, but it did not babble down over stones. It was as still as a pool. And yet the water sound continued.

They heard the voice again, like the purr of a big cat in a barrel.

'There he is,' whispered Hal, pointing.

'What a whopping big fellow,' Roger whispered.

The great black fellow sat on his haunches at the edge of the stream. He was drinking, but not the way an animal drinks. Nearly every sort of animal drinks by putting its mouth down into the water. He drank like a man, first brushing away the leaves and twigs that lay on the surface. Then, instead of lowering his head, he scooped up the water, using his hands as a cup, and, sitting up straight, he drank.

A little of the water leaked between his fingers and splashed on the surface of the brook. That explained the tinkling or dripping sound the men had heard.

The black shadow, done with drinking, stood up. He towered almost seven feet tall.

'This fellow must be five feet around,' whispered Hal. 'I'll bet he weighs seven hundred pounds if he weighs an ounce.'

The monster turned so they could see his profile. Now they could get a real idea of the size of that tremendous head, the beetling brows, the flat nose, the huge projecting jaws, the retreating chin.

There was no doubt about it – they were looking at a gorilla, and a great one. Most male gorillas, Hal knew from his studies, stood some five or six feet tall and weighed from five hundred to six hundred pounds. A lowland gorilla in the San Diego zoo tipped the scales at five hundred and eighty-five, and another at six hundred and eighteen.

A gorilla that had been killed in the Forest of Bambio near the Congo River in 1920 and whose photograph was published in a French scientific journal, measured nine feet four inches. But it was a freak and nothing like it had ever been heard of since.

The monster they were now looking at was the greatest living creature on two legs that they had ever seen.

'Looks like Gog,' Hal whispered.

Roger knew what he meant. In the Guildhall in London they had seen that huge wooden statue of Gog.

The legend was that there used to be a race of giants on earth. Gog was supposed to be the last of those giants. And the monster that stood before them now looked like the giant Gog. He too, perhaps, was one of the last of his race. When the remaining mountain gorillas were wiped out, there would be no more man-like giants on earth.

Hal mentally pinned the name Gog on the giant that stood before them.

He could imagine Gog walking out of the shadows into the full glare of the Ringling Circus – how ten thousand heads would lean forward, how men would gasp, how the girls would scream.

A shaft of sun broke through the clouds and brought out the monster in sharp relief. For the first time they could see that he was not all black. Down the middle of his back ran a streak of silver. Except for these almost white hairs, all the hair on his body was black and stood out as if electrified.

Why had the silverback not noticed his audience peering through the bushes? The average animal would have seen them or heard them or smelled them. But not the gorilla. That was another thing that made him like man. The gorilla is as clever as man in some ways, but also as stupid as man. His senses of sight, hearing, and smell are neither better nor worse than man's.

But in size and strength, thought Hal, this giant left man far behind. How would they capture him? Four men certainly could not do it. It was a job for the whole crew. He started back towards the trail and the others followed. They must move fast – their prize might wander away before they could bring the crew.

Once on the trail, they broke into a dog-trot. Roger was so busy glancing left and right that he almost stumbled.

'Watch your step,' Tieg said.

'I was wondering where his family is,' Roger said. 'I'll bet it's near by.'

Another ten minutes of running, then Roger said, 'See that open spot under the big trees? I'm going to sidetrack and take a look at it. Then I'll catch up with you.'

He dodged into the bushes and a moment later called, 'Come back. Here it is.' The others joined him. They crept up quietly, but there was no need of that. Here was the family, but they were not waiting for their lord's return.

Two females and a half-grown male lay on the ground,

quite dead. Their bodies were still warm. Blood trickled from spear wounds.

From far away in the jungle came a high-pitched scream. 'Baby gorilla,' Joro guessed.

He examined the ground. It was trampled with footprints – and these footprints were human.

It was not difficult to figure out what had happened. A gang of Africans had attacked the family, hoping to take the baby alive. The other members of the family had desperately defended the youngster and so had met their death. Three animals had been killed to capture one.

If there had been four hundred gorillas in the Virunga country, now there were only three hundred and ninety-seven. There were strict laws against killing these animals. Scores of other animal species had disappeared from the face of the earth because they had been hunted to the death by man. If this sort of murder went on, the mountain gorilla would join the gone and forgotten.

4
The Bullet

The native gang had evidently made off with the baby of the family. Why?

'Why didn't they take a big one?' Roger wondered.

'Perhaps they didn't know how,' Hal said. 'It was easier to kill the large ones, then grab the baby.'

'But if they intend to sell it they won't get as much for it,' Roger said.

'Ten thousand dollars. The same price as for a big one.'

'That doesn't make sense,' Roger objected.

'Yes it does. Figure it out for yourself. If you were running a zoo, which would you rather have – a big gorilla that would perhaps last only ten years more, or a little one that you could have on exhibit for its full life-span of thirty years?'

'Well,' said Roger, 'I'd like to have both – a big one so that people could see what a giant gorilla looks like, and a little one that would live a long time.'

'Exactly. That's why they're worth the same money.'

'Okay,' Roger said. 'But here's another puzzle. Why

is it forbidden to kill gorillas but you can get a permit to take them alive?'

'Because a dead gorilla is one gorilla less in the world. But if you take a live gorilla and put it in a zoo you haven't reduced the number of gorillas. In fact, you are doing the gorillas a favour – because they live better and live longer in a well-kept zoo than they would in the jungle where they have so many enemies. Some people say that animals pine away in a zoo. That's true in some cases – but generally it's the other way round – the animal is not at all unhappy to be safe and well-fed, cured of his diseases if he has any, and entertained by watching the funny humans who come to look at him.'

'Listen,' Roger said.

There was a crackling in the bushes, then out stepped the giant they had seen beside the stream. He was still talking to himself in a low, contented voice.

He stopped short when he saw what had happened to his family. Then his voice changed to an agonized *aoo, aoo, aoo*. He ran forward and stooped over the body of the young male, probably his son. Then he dropped between his two wives. With his great hands he tried to stop the blood that still trickled from their wounds. He shook them as if trying to bring them back to consciousness. Then he put one great hairy arm around each, drew them close to him and rocked back and forth, moaning pitifully.

Suddenly there was a change. The giant dropped the two warm dead bodies and leaped to his feet. He looked all about him and one could guess the thought in his mind, 'Who did this?'

His eyes came to rest on the men not too well concealed in the bushes. He let out a blood-curdling scream that echoed back from the crags of Karisimbi, the next volcano. It was so chilling a sound that it numbed the nerves and the men stood as if paralysed.

Gog beat upon the ground with the palms of his hands. What hands! Each as big as a baseball glove. He began to walk towards the men, bellowing as he came, and slapping the great drum of his chest.

The men stood like statues, their hearts thumping. Their first impulse was to turn and run. But they knew very well that this would only invite an attack. Their only chance was to stand firm and out-bluff the beast.

If he behaved in true gorilla fashion he would come within perhaps ten feet of them, then stop, and turn aside.

But the giant Gog did not stick to the rules of the

game. His natural fear of man was wiped out by his rage and grief over the slaughter of his family.

The expression on the monster's face was enough to chill your blood. It was not just because the wide-open mouth showed teeth as big as a lion's. The face was terrible because it was so like the face of a man when he is in a deadly rage.

Hal and Roger had been charged by other animals, and that was bad enough, but this was more terrifying. A charging rhino's face is completely without expression. The features of the buffalo are the same whether he is nibbling grass or coming to kill. A hippo may be full of fury but his pig-like eyes don't show it. A charging elephant spreads his ears and raises his trunk, but there is no change in his face. The face of a charging lion, except for his open jaws, is calm and ordinary. So it is throughout the animal kingdom – until you come to the great apes. They alone, and that other animal, man, have a face that can truly express their emotions.

But even man, no matter how angry, does not smell like an angry gorilla. A slight breeze brought the odour to Roger's nostrils.

'He smells like burning rubber,' Roger said.

Gog spread his huge hairy arms so that no one

might escape him. The arm reach was a good eight feet. The shoulder muscles heaved and it was clear that one of those enormous hands could twist a man's head off.

The hairs on the ape's forehead twitched up and down and Roger felt the hair on his own neck do something like it.

Tieg's huge body was trembling like a leaf. This was actually the first mountain gorilla he had ever seen. All he had told the boys about gorillas he had picked up from men who had hunted them. He knew nothing about them first-hand.

So it was natural for him to do the wrong thing.

He bent down, grabbed a rock, and threw it with all his strength.

It struck the monster full in the chest but had no more effect upon him than if he had been struck by a feather.

The ape picked it up and threw it back. That again reminded the boys of the stories about the great Gog who fought by hurling rocks at his enemies.

The rock caught Tieg in the stomach and doubled him up.

The gorilla did not stop at ten feet nor at five feet nor

at one. A sideways slap of his left arm laid Roger and Joro flat on the ground and his right arm did the same for Hal.

He reserved special treatment for Tieg. He picked up the big fellow and flung him into a tree where he landed on a branch twelve feet up, then fell to the ground.

Tieg drew a revolver and fired.

The bullet found its mark but did not fell the beast. He clutched his shoulder, then turned and disappeared into the woods.

Hal bent over the unconscious body of Roger. He felt his pulse, made sure the boy was breathing.

'He'll come round,' he said and, sure enough, after a few minutes Roger opened his eyes and inquired weakly, 'What happened to me?'

His tough young body survived a blow that would have killed someone who had not been hardened as Roger had been by many adventures in the African bush.

The men picked themselves up and stumbled in a sort of daze along the path towards the cabin. Hal looked curiously at Tieg.

'I thought you said not to carry a gun.'

Tieg was embarrassed. 'Oh, that,' he said. 'Well, you see, I thought it was just an extra precaution.'

'But I thought you said you weren't afraid of gorillas.'

'Afraid? Who's afraid? I just thought I ought to be ready to protect you in case of trouble. You were very lucky that I did bring it along. I saved your lives and I expect a little gratitude for that.'

Hal smiled and let the big coward enjoy his feeling of self-importance.

Roger kept glancing back. After he had done this several times his brother asked, 'What's the matter, kid?'

'I have a nasty feeling that we're being followed.'

Hal looked back but could see nothing – nothing but trees. Perhaps his brother was imagining things. Perhaps he was still suffering from the shock of having been knocked unconscious by one swipe of the great Gog's mighty arm.

They came out into the clearing and walked through the flowers to the cabin. Here at last with their thirty men around them they felt safe.

Roger looked back again. 'I see him – Gog – looking through the bushes – no, I don't – yes I do – no I don't.'

'Get hold of yourself,' Hal said. 'Your nerves are all

in a tangle. With that bullet in him Gog is still running. He's probably miles away by this time.'

But he wasn't too sure about it. As they entered their cabin and flopped down on the camp beds to rest, he began to wonder. Suppose the kid had really seen something. Suppose Gog had followed them and now knew where to find them. Gog believed that they had slaughtered his family. They had put a bullet in him. He had been too tough to kill, but perhaps the bullet was causing him terrible pain and added to his determination to take revenge. Perhaps they had not seen the last of Gog.

5
Pythons are Like That

Roger was restless. Every time he began to doze off he saw an angry black face in the bushes and a hairy arm five hundred feet long reaching all the way across the clearing to knock him senseless.

He woke and worried. Not just because he was afraid of Gog. But also because he was sorry for Gog. The great beast had lost his loved ones. Then Tieg had made matters worse. Now Gog, wounded and suffering, had become a deadly enemy. Half crazy with pain, he was raging through the forest ready to kill the first human he saw.

'Hal,' Roger said. 'Wake up.'

'Go to sleep.'

'Listen, Hal. We've got to do something.'

'Like what?'

'Get that bullet out of him.'

It was not the reply Hal had expected. But it was just like Roger to plan how to help an animal rather than escape from it.

'Don't talk nonsense,' Hal said. 'How can you

make friends with a beast that is bent on murdering you?'

'I don't know,' admitted Roger. 'But we've got to do it, somehow. And you've got to fire Tieg.'

'Unfortunately, we can't do that. He's under contract. We had to guarantee to keep him on until we're done with our job in these mountains. But there's one thing I can do, perhaps. Relieve him of his revolver.'

Roger laughed. 'Now there's something I'd like to see. I suppose you'll just say, "Pretty please, Mr Tieg, I'd like to have your gun."'

Hal smiled. 'Something like that,' he said.

'And if he doesn't fork it over?'

'Then I'll have to try gentle persuasion.'

Joro burst into the room.

'Python, bwana.'

'Where?'

'In the lake.'

'Keep your eye on it. We'll be right out.'

Ringling Circus wanted a python. And here was one almost at their front door. Their weariness was promptly forgotten and they ran out to the edge of the lake.

They looked in vain for the python. Joro pointed. 'There.'

They had expected to see the longest animal in Africa. All they saw was a nose. It projected above the surface just far enough to allow the creature to breathe.

It reminded him of the great serpent of the Amazon jungle, the anaconda. It was a first cousin of the python. They both belonged to the boa family. But the anaconda was a water snake, while the python was supposed to be a land snake. Yet they both had this habit of lying doggo in the water close to shore, ready to leap out and grab any animal that might come to drink.

'How do we get it out of there?' Roger wondered. 'Lasso it? Use a net?'

'It would go down before we could get a rope or a net on it,' Hal said.

'How could it go down? It has to stay up to breathe.'

'No. It can stay under and hold its breath for a good twenty minutes. In the meantime it could swim away under water and we would have no idea where to find it. We won't have much luck using force. But perhaps we can give it a good reason to come out.'

'What do you mean? Do you think you can argue with a python?'

'Yes. If we have another animal to help us.' Hal's eye roamed around the clearing. He spotted a duiker antelope grazing near the edge of the woods.

Mali, one of his men, was carrying a lasso. 'See if you can snag that duiker,' Hal said.

Mali roped the unsuspecting little antelope without difficulty.

'Bring it over here – close to the water,' Hal said.

Mali dragged the bucking, prancing little creature until it stood on the shore close to the waiting python. Mali himself disappeared into the bushes, still holding the end of the line.

There was a sudden surge of water as the snake with head raised and jaws open shot towards its prey.

'Haul in,' shouted Hal.

Mali hauled the trembling little creature into the safety of the bushes and let it go. A dozen men descended upon the great snake. Wet and slippery, it slithered through their fingers and dived into a hole. The men were disappointed.

'Never mind,' Hal said. 'We'll get it yet. It must have its nest down there. Sooner or later it will come out again. Be ready to grab it.'

They stood and waited – ten, twenty, thirty minutes.

The cook suddenly had an idea. He went to the provision truck and came back with a sprig of garlic. 'In my village,' the man said, 'they used to say that snakes liked garlic. They just can't stay away from it.' He put down the garlic at the edge of the hole. 'That will bring him out.'

Hal was too wise to laugh at such notions. This was only one of many local superstitions.

Another was that the python is sacred. Many tribes worship it as a sort of god. If you kill a python there will be no rain and your crops will die.

Another notion is that a python must have its tail locked around a tree before it throws its coils about you. Naturalists know that this is not so – many pythons have attacked men and animals on the plains where there were no trees.

Another common idea is that the snake uses its tongue as a paintbrush and covers its victim with saliva so it will slip down more easily. Actually the tongue is too small for such a job. It would be like trying to paint a barn with a toothbrush.

The snake has two small bumps underneath and is supposed to press these into its victim's nostrils so that it cannot breathe. This is not true, but the truth is more strange. The two bumps are the remains of feet. Some millions of years ago snakes walked.

One more popular idea is that no snake dies before sundown. This is not the case, but there is some reason for such a superstition as the boys were soon to find out.

The rainbow, in the traditions of some tribes, is an enormous python coiled around the globe, and only the most powerful witch doctors can keep it from squeezing the world to death.

The garlic didn't work. But something was working. Hal, standing about twenty feet away from the hole, began to feel the earth moving beneath him. Hal was not surprised, because this part of Africa, peppered with volcanoes, was subject to violent earthquakes.

A sudden upheaval made him stagger off to more solid ground.

What a strange earthquake that was. No one else seemed to have felt anything. No tree showed the least tremor. The earthquake had been under him and nowhere else.

6
Wrestling Match

The earth squirmed and broke and there was the thrashing tail of the python. It seemed as if the snake, instead of being attracted by the garlic, was trying to get as far away from it as possible.

The tail was beginning to go down again. Hal grabbed it and shouted to the men to come and help.

They took hold and began to pull. But a snake knows very well what to do in a case like that. It braces itself against the walls of the hole. The muscles swell and turn rigid, locking the body firmly in place.

But if the snake could play tricks, Hal could do the same. He knew the snake would try to go deeper and escape. To do so, it must release its grip on the sides of the hole.

'Don't keep up a steady pull,' Hal said. 'Now, let up a bit.' The men stopped pulling. Immediately the python loosened its hold and started down. 'Now, pull!' Hal shouted. The men heaved back and the snake instead of going forward as planned, lost ten or twelve inches. Once more it gripped the sides and could be pulled no farther.

Again Hal said, 'Let up.' The men stopped pulling. The snake relaxed its hold and started down. 'Pull,' Hal ordered, and out came another foot or so of snake.

Again and again the stratagem was repeated. But now there was a new difficulty. The more of the writhing body that was pulled out, the more difficult it was to control the struggling reptile.

More men were called to help. Now the big snake had thirty men to reckon with. The contorting snake flung them back and forth, bruising them against the trees, shaking them off repeatedly – for the python has no convenient handles by which it may be held.

Presently out came a bulge: something the serpent had swallowed and had not yet digested. Then another bulge. Evidently the creature had breakfasted well that morning.

And now the head itself appeared. It was about half the size of either of the bulges. How could a snake swallow something twice the size of its own head?

The secret lay in its jaws. They are not hinged as ours are. They are connected by something like elastic bands. They can be stretched apart to take in an animal the size of a calf.

Hal and Roger had previously seen a python that had

swallowed a red deer – all but the horns. They projected weirdly from the sides of the mouth. But this time the bulges were smaller, only about a foot in diameter, and their nature remained a mystery.

With a violent twist the snake threw off the men who had locked their arms around its neck and turned on one of its enemies with jaws agape.

The man stumbled and fell. The snake acted swiftly. Its teeth closed on the man's bare shoulder.

The python has no poison fangs. But the sharp powerful teeth can inflict a serious wound. Its long teeth are as sharp as needles. They are curved in like fish-hooks so that once they have taken hold they do not let go.

The men forgot the tail and tried to rescue their companion from the snake's jaws. At once the neglected tail swung round, beating down several men, then coiled about the body of the man who had been bitten. The man was Toto, one of Hal's best. He fought bravely but could do little since his arms were pinioned to his sides.

Every time he breathed out, the coils tightened. That is the constrictor's favourite method of killing. Often it does not break any bones, but merely squeezes more and more tightly so that the victim cannot breathe. When breathing has stopped the heart also will soon stop.

But don't believe it if someone tells you that a constrictor cannot break bones if it wants to. A circus performer was killed by a seventeen-foot snake and was found afterwards to have bones broken in eighty-four places.

If the snake succeeded in squeezing all the life out of Toto it would then proceed to swallow him. Whether it could do so would depend upon the size of the snake and the size of the man. There are hundreds of proven cases of the swallowing of humans by members of the boa family.

The boa constrictor, which grows only to a length of some twelve feet, cannot do it. But it is not impossible for the great anaconda or the python. A python more than thirty feet in length swallowed a grown East Indian woman. A boy fourteen years old was swallowed by a snake eighteen feet long. When a Burmese disappeared his friends searched for him, found nothing but his slippers, and nearby a gorged python twenty-five feet long. Upon opening it they found the body of their companion.

And yet a python is not a vicious creature. It almost never makes trouble unless it is attacked. It is easily tamed and many an African keeps a pet python in the house to rid the place of rats and other vermin.

Hal was already trying to pull the great jaws apart and the sharp teeth were cutting his fingers. Roger ran to the supply wagon and came back with a crowbar.

'Good!' cried Hal, seizing the bar and forcing it between the great teeth. Two men helped him pry the jaws open and free the bloody shoulder. Others had seized the tail and were uncoiling the snake from Toto's body. Toto knew nothing of all this. He had fainted.

Roger's crowbar did the trick. The jaws separated and the uncoiled serpent fell away.

But if the men thought the snake was exhausted they were mistaken. Before they realized what was happening the python plunged into one of the holes. It might stay down for hours, or even for days.

Big Tieg had been standing safely in the background. Now he saw his chance to be a hero. He came striding in among the men, who stood no higher than his shoulders. His great yellow moustache whipped about in the breeze, his glass eye stared coldly at the men, and his other eye fixed itself scornfully upon Hal.

'You've made a pretty botch of it, haven't you,' he said.

'You could have done better?' Hal inquired.

'Naturally. You seem to forget that I am the guide of this expedition. This is no job for boys.'

'If you have any plan let's hear it,' Hal said. 'The snake is frightened now. Heaven knows how long it'll stay down. If you know how to get it up, go to it.'

'Simple,' Tieg said. 'Men, get some brush and put it down that hole.' The men obeyed. 'Now set fire to the brush.' The fire was soon blazing fiercely. 'No snake can stand that. It will come out the other hole. All of you, stand close around that hole and grab it when it comes out.'

The men closed in around the hole. Perhaps Tieg was right. The python, dreading the fire, would surely try to escape by this exit.

No one happened to notice that Tieg did not join the men around the hole where the snake was expected to emerge. He stood at a safe distance by the other hole where the fire burned.

He was taken completely by surprise when straight up through the flames shot a great yellow head drawing after it a writhing black-and-brown body with two lumps. Like a thunderbolt it struck Tieg in the chest with its nose, tough as a battering ram, and threw its coils around him.

Tieg in a panic drew his revolver and fired into the creature's open mouth. The bullet passed up through the head. The snake fell away and the thirty-foot body twisted into knots in the death agony.

Hal faced Tieg. 'I'll take that gun,' he said.

'Why?'

'You knew very well we wanted to take that snake alive. You got scared and killed it. That's the second time you've gummed things up. There's a gorilla in the woods with a bullet in him because you lost your nerve. Now you can give me that gun.'

Tieg's glass eye bored a hole through Hal's head while the other eye studied him from hair to boots and up again.

'You impudent young whipper-snapper,' he said slowly. 'If you want the gun, why don't you take it?'

His height was several inches more than Hal's six feet and his cockatoo hair made him seem even taller. His shoulders were broader and his weight was greater by about fifty pounds.

But Hal, though only nineteen, was taller and stronger than his own father and his muscles were hardened by constant use. He looked much less formidable than the man with the great yellow moustache. His men pressed in, ready to back him up.

Tieg laughed. 'You'll need all the help you can get before I am done with you.'

Hal motioned to the others to stand back. 'If I have to take you on I'll do it alone,' he said. 'But I don't want to fight you. I only want that gun. There's no reason we can't be friends. But we can't get along if you shoot every animal we want to take alive. Now, give me the gun.'

'I'll give you something but it won't be the gun,' Tieg said, and landed a blow in Hal's midriff that made him stagger.

Tieg, encouraged by this success, lunged forward. Hal with the lake behind him could go back no farther. He stepped to one side, tripped Tieg with his foot and sent him flying into the lake.

Tieg disappeared completely. When he came up, dripping and furious, his moustache drooped like a wet dishrag and his formerly erect hair was plastered down on his scalp. The laughter of the men made him more angry.

'I'll get you for this,' he raged and came at his opponent like a runaway locomotive. This time Hal did not dodge. He used a bit of the karate that he had learned in Japan. He stooped under Tieg's fists, seized his ankles, and sent him soaring through the air to land head down in the python hole in the midst of the flames. Tieg's wet clothes sent up a column of steam.

Hal pulled him out of the hole and removed the gun from his holster. Tieg's adventure in water and fire had taken all the fight out of him.

'Better go and change your clothes,' Hal said.

Tieg got up and stumbled off towards the cabin.

7
Another Battle Lost

Joro slashed off the head of the dead snake with one stroke of his bush knife.

'We make medicine out of that,' he said.

Hal was quite willing to let the men use the dead snake as they pleased. They could grind the skull into a powder and sell the powder to the medicine men.

The joints of the backbone could be used by village women as a necklace to strengthen the throat – or as a belt to cure stomach-ache. In some African countries a string of python bones was supposed to protect the wearer against snakebite.

Serpent superstition goes back a long way. Moses set up an image of a Brazen Serpent that was supposed to have healing power. For five centuries it was worshipped as a sort of god. The Greek god of healing, Asclepius, carried a carved serpent wound around a staff. It is still the symbol of the medical profession.

Even today 'snake medicine' is sold in China. It is supposed to be a cure for insanity, convulsions, epilepsy, poor sight, colds, sore throat, malaria, earache, toothache, deafness, arthritis and rheuma-tism.

In Guatemala hot snake fat is used as a poultice for colds. Snake oil is well known in Puerto Rico.

Viper flesh was used as a medicine in France until 1884, and before that in London as a cure for the plague.

Rattlesnake oil was sold in the United States as a remedy for deafness, lumbago, toothache, sore throat and rheumatism. If you didn't want to drink it you could just rub it on any ailing part of your body.

'Is that snake dead or not?' Roger demanded, seeing that the headless body kept on twisting and squirming.

'Not yet,' Hal said.

'How can it keep on living with its head off?'

A snake's brain isn't just in its head. The rest is all the way down the spine. Keep away from it. If it catches you it can still squeeze the life out of you. Don't excite it. Keep your voice down.'

Roger stared at his brother. 'Are you kidding me? A snake has no ears. Even if it did, it couldn't hear after its head is gone.'

'A snake,' Hal said, 'has ears all over its body.'

'Now you are talking nonsense,' Roger protested.

'Not complete nonsense,' Hal smiled. 'They aren't

ears like ours. They don't exactly hear sounds. They feel them. Every sound makes vibrations and the snake feels the vibrations. Its nerves are very delicate. It can pick up sound waves that would be too faint or too high-pitched for you to get at all. It can even tell what direction the sound is coming from. Even the light footsteps of a rat would be enough. It can turn and grab that rat without looking for it. The snake's long body touching the ground all the way from head to tail gives it the ability to detect the slightest vibrations. It's like a seismograph that is used to record earthquakes. You remember in Japan the newspapers used to say how many earthquakes the seismograph had recorded in a day, sometimes a hundred, and we hadn't felt one of them. Every snake is a wriggling seismograph.'

'Speaking of hearing,' Roger said, 'do you hear a bell? Every time that snake twists I hear a tinkle.'

Hal laughed. 'Now you're the one who is crazy. Snakes don't tinkle.'

'This one does. Listen. Hear it? You're so good at explaining – explain that.'

Hal heard it. Even with all his training from childhood up as a practising naturalist, here was something he couldn't explain. 'You've got me there,' he admitted.

Toto, his shoulder bandaged, came to Hal. 'You want?' he said, pointing at the snake.

'No, I don't want it,' Hal said. 'You and the men can do what you like with it.'

Toto grinned his appreciation and went back to the men. Hal was a good boss. He had made a kind gift to his crew.

The men slit the underside of the body and began to strip off the skin. It was worth good money. Python hide makes excellent leather. It is waterproof, damp-proof, wear-resistant. It does not crack, chip or peel.

It was better than cowhide or goatskin. These animals, since they have legs to keep them up off the ground, do not need such tough skins. A python which must drag its two-hundred-pound body over the ground and through brush must be protected by heavy armour.

So python skin was strong and could be used in many ways. It could be turned into shoes, handbags, briefcases, luggage, upholstery, hats, belts and so on. Even cameras, fountain pens and tennis racket covers were made from it.

But the skin would spoil unless it was stripped

from the dead snake without delay. So Hal understood the haste of the crew.

When the hide had been peeled free, the body was cut open and out tumbled a fine pork dinner – two fat pigs who must have been swallowed recently and were little affected by the snake's digestive juices.

The snake had evidently been guilty of raiding some native village.

But still the tinkle was not explained. A little more cutting, and the mystery was cleared up. Out came the skeleton of a cat with a small bell on its neck. Toto took off the bell, washed it in the lake, and hung it on his neck-cord where it tinkled merrily as he worked.

'Dig that hole larger,' Hal advised the men. 'Perhaps you'll find the nest.'

Six feet down they came upon a large chamber containing a great number of leathery white eggs about four inches in diameter. They counted them. There were ninety unopened eggs and two that had been broken.

'Wonder what broke them,' Roger said.

'There's your answer,' Hal said, pointing out two baby snakes about a foot long. 'Notice the horny tooth on the end of their snouts. They use that to slit open the shell.'

The men were opening the other eggs. Coiled inside

each was a small but complete snake, its little forked tongue darting in and out.

The Africans seemed as delighted as if they had discovered gold. They carefully put every one of the ninety snakelets into a deep pan.

'What good are they?' Roger asked.

'You'll see at dinner-time.'

The big snake was cut into thick slices. A fire was made near the cabin and not only the pigs but generous steaks of python meat were baked in the embers. The tiny snakes were skewered on spears and grilled over the fire. Everyone came to the banquet with a fine appetite, including Hal and Roger.

It was the first time they had ever eaten snake. They were surprised to find it so good.

'It's like chicken,' Roger said, 'only not so dry.'

Hal said, 'I understand the cannibals like it even better than man-meat, just for that very reason – it's not so dry. A man is about sixty per cent water. But a snake is seventy-five per cent water.'

'I feel like a savage,' Roger said, 'sitting here and eating snake meat.'

'You don't need to feel that way about it,' Hal said. 'Your ancestors in Europe ate snake. It is still eaten to some extent in France – but for the benefit of persons who don't like the idea of eating snake, the meat is sold in the market as 'eel'. The Pilgrims who came over in the *Mayflower* ate snake when they ran out of other food. The pioneers who went West in covered wagons ate rattlers when they were short of other provisions. Rattlesnake meat is still canned in Florida. Here in Africa, where there are so many snakes, the people would be foolish if they didn't eat them. It's not savage. It's just common sense.'

For dessert the grilled baby snakes were served. The men popped the small snakes into their mouths and chewed up the soft bones and delicate flesh with much pleasure.

This was just a little bit more than Roger could take. He announced that he was not hungry any more. Even Hal would gladly have skipped this dessert. But his men were watching him. With a smile on the outside and a sickish feeling inside he downed one of the little wrigglers.

Back in the cabin Hal went to an old rolltop desk and began fishing through some papers, yellow with age.

'I saw something here about pythons – ah – this is it. It's a clipping from a missionary magazine, *Glad Tidings*, published fifty years ago. It gives some curious

advice on what to do if you are attacked by a python.'
He read the clipping:

'Remember not to run away – the python can move faster. The thing to do is to lie flat on the ground on your back with your feet together, arms to the sides and head well down. The python will then try to push its head under you, experimenting at every possible point. Keep calm. One wriggle and he will get under you, wrap his coils around you, and crush you.

'After a time the snake will get tired of this and will probably decide to swallow you without squeezing you first. He will very likely begin with one of your feet. Keep calm. You must let him swallow your foot; it is quite painless and will take a long time.

'If you lose your head and struggle, he will quickly whip his coils around you. If you keep calm, he will go on swallowing. Wait patiently until he has swallowed about up to your knee. Then carefully take out your knife and insert it into the distended side of his mouth, and with a quick rip, slit him up.'

Roger grinned. 'I don't think I could be that patient – to keep calm and let him swallow me up to the knee before I slit him up. I'd slit him up before he got that far.'

'Right,' Hal agreed. 'Only in our case we can't slit him up – nor shoot him.' He took out Tieg's gun, put it into a drawer of the desk, locked the drawer and put the key in his pocket. 'The next python we meet we've got to take alive.'

8
Roger's Luck

Roger was blue. They had failed twice. 'Wonder what boner we'll pull next,' he said bitterly.

Hal gave him no comfort. He too was disappointed.

'Well, at least,' he said, 'we've had three grand successes.'

'Oh, is that so? Tell me what they are.'

'We've succeeded in making three deadly enemies in two days. That takes real talent.'

'What enemies?'

'Gog is one. Tieg is another.'

'That's two. What's the third?'

'The mate of the python Tieg killed. We haven't heard from it yet. But we probably will.'

'Do you think a python really cares about its mate?'

'Certainly. Especially if they've been raising a family. A python can become savage if anyone interferes with its young. It has a built-in instinct to coil around its eggs and protect them until they hatch.'

'Then why wasn't there any snake coiled around the eggs when the men opened the nest?'

'Probably out foraging for food. Even a python must eat. But when it comes back and finds that its eggs have been stolen, look out. It will attack anything or anybody within reach.' He thought a moment. 'That's our chance to catch it. I'll post a man near the nest with a police whistle. If he sees the snake he can whistle us down to help him take it.'

Roger said, 'Let me do it.'

Hal smiled indulgently. His kid brother certainly had plenty of nerve. And strength too – large for his age and well supplied with muscle. But he was certainly not a match for an angry python. Suppose the snake attacked before the men could come to his aid.

'I'd rather you wouldn't,' he said. 'I'll tell Joro to pick a man for the job.'

'Why do that when you've already got a man,' Roger objected, 'or a reasonable imitation of one. There's nothing dangerous about it. All I have to do is to whistle.'

Reluctantly, Hal consented. After all, a boy must grow up. And he wouldn't grow up unless he was given responsibility.

'Go ahead. Here's the whistle. Blow loud and clear if you see anything.'

Roger took the whistle. Also he took up a coil of rope.

'What's that for?' Hal asked,

'Just to noose it if it tries to make off into the jungle before the men get there.'

He went off in high spirits. The sun had almost left the clearing. Soon it would be shut off by the tall trees. Then the animals would be coming out to drink. The python too, perhaps.

Hal, a bit anxious, watched him go to the other side of the lake. Then he went out and found Joro.

'My brother is watching for the python's mate,' he said. 'If he sees it he will blow his whistle. When you hear it, get down there in a hurry. Tell the men.'

Roger scanned the lake, but there was no sign of a python. He looked down the hole that had been enlarged to get at the eggs. He examined the other hole. He could not see very far down – the snake might or might not be at home. Or it might be out looking for food, or prowling in search of those who had taken its mate.

Roger hid in the bushes. He tried to keep still in spite of the mosquitoes that found his blood so refreshing.

The forest dwellers began to come out for their evening drink. An impala, stepping daintily, was first.

Then came two bushbuck and a topi. Two gorgeous white-and-black colobus monkeys came out, earnestly discussing something between themselves, drank, then, still arguing, disappeared into the forest.

Not all the creatures were forest animals. A giraffe, probably from the open valley between Mounts Mikeno and Karisimbi, was the next visitor. It could not reach the water with its long neck because its legs were longer. It had to spread its feet far apart in order to bring its body low enough so that its muzzle could touch the water.

A lion passing close by caught Roger's scent and stopped. It looked at him long and hard, growling softly. But when Roger did not move it decided to let well enough alone and went on to the water's edge.

When it came back it stopped again. Roger did not move a finger. The lion shook its head as if to say, 'You know I could, if I wanted to,', then plodded back into the woods.

The bushes parted and a great gorilla lumbered out. Roger's heart beat faster. Perhaps this was Gog. It stopped to look him over. No, its features were not like Gog's – Roger was to learn that no two gorillas look the same. Like people, every one is a bit different. This one's great face was blue-black, and there was no white streak down the back. And it would not stand there so calmly if it were being tortured by a bullet wound. It cupped its hands and began to slap its great chest. But it was quite half-hearted about it, for it was not accompanied by its family, and this other ape with clothes on showed no fear. So it dropped its football-sized hands to the ground, knuckles down, and went on to the lake.

What a specimen – and Roger was letting it slip through his fingers. He burned with a desire to throw his noose and lasso this prize. But what then? The gorilla could turn on him and tear him to pieces. He could blow his whistle, but the gorilla had far more sense than the python – it would be gone before the men could arrive. Aching with frustration, Roger let ten thousand dollars walk by.

Something was happening at one of the python holes. A white nose was emerging. It couldn't be the nose of a python, because the African python has a yellow and black head and a black or dark-brown body spotted with light-brown designs.

But this thing was white. It looked more like the nose of a polar bear. Of course that was absurd. What could it be?

Now the whole head was up and out. Roger could see

plainly by the shape of the head that it was a python – but snow-white with blue eyes. A red tongue darted in and out. The tongue, instead of being a stinger as many people supposed, was a sort of miniature radar outfit. Every snake was so equipped, whether poisonous or non-poisonous. Roger knew this very well, but still could not help being a bit nervous when he saw a snake's darting tongue.

Another foot or two of the gleaming white snake emerged.

It was time to act. Roger put the whistle to his mouth. But no, he must not blow it yet – the snake would feel the sound and escape. Roger must first get the lasso over the head. Then he would blow for all he was worth.

It was necessary to step out of the bushes to get room to swing his rope. The snake, startled by his sudden appearance, raised its head.

Roger swung the lasso and let fly. The noose dropped over the head and neck and was drawn tight. The snake immediately whipped out of the hole and twisted itself into knots in an effort to get rid of the noose.

Now was the time to blow that whistle. But as Roger was bringing it to his mouth something new and exciting happened. The gorilla, returning from the water's edge,

in the uncertain light of dusk managed to step on a coil of the writhing snake.

Immediately the angry serpent threw its tail around the gorilla's legs and its head darted upward in a spiral that wrapped the gorilla's arms tightly to its sides and brought snake and ape face to face. The python's jaws closed on the gorilla's shoulder.

Roger acted swiftly. He leaped forward and whipped the rope round and round the two struggling forms. He was about to tie the end of the line to a tree. But he saw that this was not necessary. The gorilla's feet were locked together. It could not take a single step.

The mighty arms might easily have broken the snake's backbone if they had been free. But they too were locked.

The snake was constricting now. Every time the ape exhaled the coils tightened. No ordinary animal could stand this. The breath would be squeezed out of it and the heart would stop.

Roger, fearing that the gorilla would cave in and die, blew a lusty blast on his whistle.

Immediately there was a commotion at the cabin. The men burst out and came running, Hal in the lead.

If Hal expected to see his brother in the coils of the

python, he was much relieved to find Roger sitting calmly on a rock looking out over the quiet lake. Near him, as still as a monument, stood a hairy monster wrapped in python and rope.

'You'd better untwist them,' Roger said, 'before the ape gets all the life pinched out of it.'

Hal examined the monument. 'I don't think you need worry. Any ordinary animal would be dead by this time. But that rib cage is too stout to be crushed by any python.'

'Then you're not going to pull them apart?'

'No. You've made a very neat package of them. I'd say you couldn't have done it better if you had had them gift-wrapped. If we separate them, then we'll have trouble with both of them. We'll take them just as they are. Mali, go get a net.'

When the net came it was wrapped quickly around both figures then tied fast.

'Lay hold,' Hal said, but the men stood back. Hal guessed the reason. The very rare white python is especially sacred. There is a tradition that the goddess Hali returns as a white snake every thousand years.

'She will bring us disaster if we don't treat her kindly,' Toto said.

'We'll treat her very kindly,' Hal assured him. 'Any man who harms her will be punished. Come, take hold.'

Hal himself gripped the net near the upper end of the two-headed monster. Other men, encouraged by his example, hesitantly stepped forward and slipped their fingers through the stout meshes of the net. There was no room for more than ten men, five on each side.

Hal, whose scientific mind reduced facts to figures whenever possible, estimated that this number of hands would be enough. The gorilla must weigh five hundred pounds or more, and the snake added another two hundred. That made seven hundred pounds, or seventy for each of ten men. That shouldn't be too much for anyone.

And yet it was not easy, for both animals began to struggle when they were tipped to a horizontal position and carried towards the camp. The snake released the gorilla's shoulder and tried to get at Hal, but was baffled by the net. Hal examined the ape's shoulder and was glad to find that the heavy hair and tough hide had resisted the sharp teeth of the python. A bite that would have sunk an inch deep in a human shoulder had not even drawn blood.

He could not believe his good luck. Two of the animals

they had most wanted were in that net. They had not been so much as scratched in the taking. They were both perfect specimens, and the snake was super-perfect. A white python was as rare as a snowball in a hot place.

The men who were not occupied as bearers were chattering in Swahili and looking at Roger. He could understand only enough of what they were saying to know that it wasn't bad. Suddenly they seized him, hoisted him to their shoulders and bore him along in triumph.

'Let me down,' he demanded, but for once they refused to obey him. They did not set down the much embarrassed boy until they reached the trucks.

Under Hal's orders, a large cage on one of the trucks was opened and, to Roger's great surprise, both animals were placed inside.

'Surely not both in one cage,' he objected.

'Why not?' Hal said. 'They'll be company for each other.'

'They'll fight and one of them will be killed.'

'No, I don't think so. You've already seen that the python can't do a thing to the gorilla. And when a gorilla isn't defending its family it's generally good-natured. I think they'll actually need each other.'

'Need each other, my eye! What do a snake and an ape have in common?'

'Companionship,' Hal said. 'A solitary gorilla is apt to die of lonesomeness. That's why there are only thirteen mountain gorillas in all the zoos of the world. They must have something to interest them. The best thing would be another gorilla, and perhaps we'll get one. But until we do, the python may be enough to keep her interested.'

'Her?'

'Yes. They're both ladies. And we'll have to treat them as ladies should be treated. The first thing is to get them out of that net.'

He climbed into the cage and let down the door, shutting himself in with his two visitors, either one of which was quite capable of hugging him to death.

He took out his bush knife and slit the heavy strands of the net from top to bottom and got out again before the animals realized they were no longer bound. They disentangled themselves slowly. There was nothing to excite or disturb them, except that they were in unfamiliar surroundings. The gorilla retreated to one corner and the snake to another and each pretended to be completely uninterested in the other.

'It will take them a little time to get used to being room-mates,' Hal said.

The two watched each other suspiciously, but without fear. The snake was not afraid of the gorilla. Gorillas do not eat snakes but dine on fruit, bark, bamboo shoots and herbs. The gorilla was not afraid of the snake. The python's coils that could squeeze the life out of a lion were not strong enough to crush the great ape's chest.

There was no reason, Hal thought, why they should not get along together.

Discussing the matter at bedtime, the brothers agreed it had been a great day. 'Thanks to you,' Hal said.

Roger would not accept the compliment. 'I didn't do a thing. They just captured each other. It was pure luck.'

'Not exactly,' Hal said. 'You used your head. You took a rope with you. Tieg would have taken a gun. When the gorilla showed up you could have lassoed it. That would be the wrong thing to do. The gorilla would certainly have attacked you, and perhaps killed you. You noosed the python. You might have whistled then, but we couldn't have got there before the snake would have had you. When the snake got stepped on and attacked the gorilla, you still didn't blow your whistle. If you had, they would probably have separated and attacked you.

That would have been two against one, and you never could have lived through it. Instead, you roped them together – and then blew your whistle. It was all good timing.'

'I still say it was luck,' Roger said. 'The gorilla came along at just the right second. I'm going to call her Lady Luck.'

'And how about the other lady?'

'Snow White,' suggested Roger.

'Snow White it is,' Hal agreed. 'That will distinguish her from an albino.'

'But she is an albino.'

'No. An albino usually isn't pure white. You can still see faint markings on the skin. Besides, an albino has pink eyes. The eyes of this python are blue.'

'If she isn't an albino, what is she?'

'A sport.'

'What's a sport?'

'Well, you might say it's a freak. Something completely different from the usual. Every circus is eager to get a few sports to amaze the public – a woman with long whiskers, a horse with two heads, anything that people will pay good money to see. Often a sport is ugly. But this one is beautiful. That's an added attraction.'

'I'll bet they've never seen as pretty a snake as Snow White.'

'Not for many years, anyhow,' Hal said. 'When I was a youngster and you hadn't been born yet, an animal collector called Ryhiner went about the country exhibiting a white python he called Serata – it's a Sanskrit word that means "beauty". I remember seeing her on a purple cushion with gold fringes in the window of Swissair at Rockefeller Center. She attracted so many people that the police had to be called out to control traffic. Ryhiner was offered fifteen thousand dollars for her but refused. Prices have gone up a lot since then. Do you realize that your Snow White is worth at least twenty thousand – and your ape another ten thousand? A pretty good day's work.'

Roger tried to be properly happy about this improvement in the family fortunes, but the thought of parting with either one of his two new friends was a bit sad. He had a way with animals – they trusted him, and were easily tamed. But what was the use of getting new friends if you couldn't keep them?

Before going to bed he picked up his flashlight and slipped out to see how the two new members of the expedition were faring. He was not quite prepared for what he saw. Lady Luck was stretched out sound asleep, and Snow White had crept over and lay snuggled close against the warm-blooded creature, almost covered by the gorilla's shaggy hair.

They would get along.

9
Massacre

Roger's capture OF the gorilla and the white python seemed a happy promise of future success.

Instead, it was the beginning of trouble.

Everything went wrong. Roger, creeping out at dawn to see how his guests were doing, found that someone or something had been tampering with the padlock on the cage door. It still held, but it was bent and battered.

If the night had been a little longer or the tools a little stronger, Roger would now be looking into an empty cage.

Joro came out. Roger called him over. 'Look at this,' Roger said, and Joro examined the lock.

'What do you make of it?' Roger queried. 'Was it done with a hammer? Or a pair of pincers?'

'We would have heard hammering,' Joro said. 'It could have been done with pincers. But it looks more like a bite.'

Roger stared. 'That's a pretty wild guess, isn't it?'

Joro grinned. 'Pretty wild,' he admitted. 'But look.

On both sides, the dents are in a curve as if they had been made by teeth. No pincers could do that.'

'But how could teeth do it?' Roger objected. 'Nobody has teeth that strong. That's a good solid iron lock.'

Joro shook his head. 'It just looks that way. I can't explain it. I can't imagine who or what could have done it. A hyena will even chew up a tin can. But a lock would be too much for it. A lion or leopard has strong teeth. But they have no taste for hardware.'

Hal came out and joined the investigators. The others said nothing but waited for him to express an opinion. He studied the lock, then the iron grille on each side of it and above and below.

'This was done by something pretty intelligent,' he said. 'Any ordinary animal, a rhino for example, would have just banged around hit and miss, trying to get through the grille. But you see no marks anywhere except on the lock. Whatever did this could have been watching from the bushes when we put the animals into the cage. He saw us apply the lock and realized it was the thing to go after if he wanted to get the cage open.'

'So you think it was done by an animal?' asked Roger.

'I didn't say that. I just say that if it was done by an animal, it must have been an intelligent animal. But it could have been done by a not too intelligent human with some sort of tool that didn't do a good job.'

Joro's eyes narrowed. 'Are you implying that one of my men could have done it?'

'No, I'm not. I have too much faith in our crew.'

'But there's no one else around.'

'They may be closer than you think,' Hal said. 'Don't forget the gang that murdered Gog's family.'

'What would they have against us?'

'They were probably after Gog too. But they couldn't sell him with a bullet in him. They blame us for that. Then you bag a big female. There aren't too many gorillas around – and we've spoiled their chances to get two of them. We'll spoil a lot more of their chances if we can – they know that. So perhaps they've decided to take the easy way out. Let us do the hard work of capturing the animals and then steal them from us. I don't know. It's just a guess.'

Tieg appeared, twirling his big yellow moustache. 'And there's one more guess,' Hal said. 'Joro, say nothing about it to the men, but I want you to keep your eye on Tieg. The commandant told us that he was broke. What a temptation to try and get away with specimens worth thirty thousand. Mind, I'm not accusing him. Just keep your eye on him, that's all.'

After a hasty breakfast the boys, with Tieg and twenty of the crew, set out on a scouting trip through the surrounding forest to see if they could locate the enemy gang. Ten men were left to guard Lady Luck and Snow White.

Where the gang had attacked Gog's family they were surprised to find – Gog himself. The wind was against them – the gorilla did not detect their presence. He was occupied with his own thoughts.

He had given his wives and son a gorilla burial by covering them thickly with branches and leaves. Now he sat near the graves with his great head bowed. He rocked back and forth, moaning softly.

'I didn't know they cared so much,' Roger whispered.

'Of course they do,' Hal said. 'Strange that such a big brute of an animal should be so affectionate. It just shows you can't go by appearances. In the zoos they have found out that they have to treat the gorilla very gently. His feelings are very easily hurt. You never punish a pet gorilla by striking him. It may not hurt him in the least, but it makes him so unhappy that he may die.'

'But sometimes they have to be punished, don't they?'

'Of course. But all you have to do is raise your voice a little and he knows he is being scolded. You don't even need to do that. Just push him away gently and he takes the hint. But you must make friends with him again very quickly or he will be physically ill. What's the matter? You look as if you had lost two wives yourself.'

'I sure am sorry for the old guy,' Roger said. 'How do you think he would take it if I went in there and tried to comfort him?'

'I think he'd take your head off. Don't forget, he still pins all his troubles on us.'

He turned to rejoin the men. Unluckily he stepped on a twig that snapped under his foot. Instantly Gog leaped to his feet. He came forward, brushing aside the bushes to get a better look. 'Stand still,' Hal said.

It didn't work this time. When Gog saw who his visitors were, a fuse seemed to light in his brain. His face, so gentle and sad a moment ago, was contorted with rage, his eyes glared out of deep black caves and his great savage mouth split open to let out an ear-splitting *uuua, uuua,* that made iced water run down the boys' spines.

Gog tore up a young tree by the roots and lumbered forward, banging his breast with one palm and brandishing the tree like a great club in his other hand.

The boys forgot all they had learned about how to behave when attacked by an angry gorilla. They turned and ran for their lives. They knew this beast was not merely angry, he was bent on murder. Fortunately for them, Gog's tree was caught in the underbrush and before he could pull it free all his enemies had disappeared.

'We should have brought a net,' Roger said, remembering his bold plan to capture Gog and get that tormenting bullet out of his body. And now, when they had had a chance to do just that, they were unprepared. Instead, the angry beast had scared the living daylights out of them.

'How could we know we would meet Gog?' Hal said. 'We didn't come out to hunt gorillas this morning. We're trying to spot that gang. Joro, do you see any tracks?'

'The ground is too hard to show tracks,' Joro said.

A half hour later it was their noses, not their eyes, that gave them some important information.

It was not a good smell. It was the smell of death and rotting flesh. Joro stood still, sniffing the air like an animal. 'Over that way,' he said, motioning to the right. They picked their way through the underbrush, then went down through a grove of ferns that in this climate grow to a height of twenty feet. The smell became stronger. The tree ferns thinned out into an open space.

Here again it was gorillas they found, not gangsters. But the gorillas were dead. Jackals that had been feeding upon the bodies ran yelping into the woods, and vultures rose in a cloud.

This had not been a single gorilla family, but a tribe. Hal counted sixty bodies of adult males and females. There were estimated to be about four hundred mountain gorillas in the region of the Virunga volcanoes. The loss of sixty was a serious matter.

There were no dead babies. They had been taken alive after the older apes had been killed. Not every gangster had escaped the angry adults. Two Africans lay dead.

Roger picked up something that was not African. He showing it to Hal. It was a small notebook full of figures and scribbled notes – in English!

'It seems to be a sort of account book. It tells where catches were made, how many were taken, cost of shipment, receipts in dollars or pounds. And here's a name on the flyleaf. It seems to be "J. J. Nero".'

Roger looked over the field of the dead. 'Do you suppose he's back of this whole thing?'

'More than likely. I hope we have a chance to deliver this notebook to Mr Nero in person.'

'Then what would you do?'

'Invite him down to see the authorities. I'll bet he has no permit for what he's doing. He ought to be put away.'

'If he goes to jail, will that stop the killing?'

'Chances are it will. The gang doesn't kill for fun. If there's nobody to pay them, why keep on? No pay, no work.'

'Look,' Roger said. 'Two live babies.'

The two youngsters had been lying unseen close to their dead mother. Now one of them sat up and the other climbed on its mother's chest, took the long hair in its two little hands and tugged vigorously. When it did not get any response it sat mournfully looking about, making no sound. A chimp would have been chattering. But gorillas are not talkative and an infant is no cry-baby.

'They look mighty lonesome,' Roger said. 'And they must be hungry. Do you think they would let me pick them up?'

'If anybody can do it, you can,' Hal said. 'You get

along well with the beasties, I don't know why. I think you must be part beastie yourself.'

'Thanks for the compliment,' Roger said. He picked his way over the bodies. He stood looking down at the two small apes and they returned his gaze without stirring. They were too young to know how dangerous a human being is.

Roger stooped beside them. They inspected him soberly. After a moment he put out his hand. He let it lie quietly between them where they could both sniff at it. He spoke to them in a low voice. His words would mean nothing to them but the gentleness of his voice was easily understood.

Slowly he moved his hand and petted one of them, then the other. They seemed to like it.

Still, he knew he couldn't rush matters. He did not attempt to take them up. Instead, he rose slowly and started to walk away. He turned and found them following close upon his heels.

He had been elected. From now on, he was their mother.

He stooped again. One of them clambered up on his shoulder and the other he took into his arms.

'A neat job,' Hal said.

10
The Honey Bird

Hal showed the notebook to Joro. 'Where do you suppose we could find this Nero?'

'Perhaps he and his whole gang would be at Kala village today,' Joro said. 'One of my scouts brings back word that they're having a big ceremony there in honour of a new chief.'

'Let's go and see,' Hal said.

Tieg was pouting. He was supposed to be the guide of this expedition but it was Joro who was leading the party. Tieg felt left out. He must assert himself. He must do something to make these people think he was a great guy – that he knew something about these woods.

But he didn't know enough to recognize a honey bird when he saw one. It sat on a branch, fluttering its wings and chirping loudly.

'It's trying to attract our attention,' Hal said. 'If we'd follow it it would lead us to some honey. But we won't take the time for that now.'

Tieg saw his chance to be important. 'It would be time well spent,' he objected. 'All of us would like some honey.

I'll go and get it for you. I'll meet you at the village later.'

Everybody in Africa knew about the honey bird. Even Tieg had heard of it, though he had never actually seen one. The honey bird, or honey guide as it was sometimes called, loved wild honey, but didn't enjoy being stung by the bees. Therefore it would guide a man to the nest in the hope that the man would get it down, scare away the bees, take some of the honey, and leave the rest for the honey guide. This was important to the little bird, because it cared for nothing so much as honey.

There was another extraordinary thing about the honey guide. If honey were not left for it, it would take revenge. Many hunters had suffered because of this peculiar habit. The angry bird would lead you again – but this time not to a bees' nest, but to a serpent or lion or leopard or some other dangerous creature, in the hope that you would be scratched, bitten or stung.

Some people, like Tieg, who had not studied the honey guide, did not believe all this. This co-operation between a man and a bird was too strange to be true. They did not realize that symbiosis, which means teamwork between two different kinds of animals, is not uncommon in nature.

The rhino and the egret are friends, the bird rides on

the beast's back and gobbles up the insects that annoy the rhino.

The tick-bird performs a similar service for the buffalo, picking out the ticks that have burrowed into the animal's hide.

The crocodile bird fearlessly enters the open mouth of the crocodile to pick bits of food from between the teeth. Also it eats the leeches that infest the creature's body. The crocodile is a bad-tempered reptile, but has a soft spot in its heart for this bird.

A small fish swims about among the arms of the sea anemone. Those arms are covered with stingers but the little fish is not stung, because it is the anemone's good friend and assistant. It tempts big fish which rush in to take it, and are promptly stung and swallowed by the anemone.

There were dozens of other examples of symbiosis, all unknown to big Tieg.

With a noisy *cher-cher-cher* the little brown-bodied, white-tailed honey guide fluttered farther away and Tieg followed. The bird impatiently waited for him to catch up, fluttering and twittering constantly, then moving on.

Presently Tieg noticed that he was not the only one following the honey guide. The other was an animal about two and a half feet long and a foot high with long sharp claws. This was the famous honey badger or ratel. He also loved honey. Honey badger and honey guide were glad to work together.

Tieg hurried. He must not let this animal beat him to the feast of honey.

The bird had now stopped going forward and was circling round and round a branch that cradled a large nest. Tieg smacked his lips. This was going to be good. The tree was not hard to climb. He clambered up the trunk and out on the branch.

Bees are not fools. They saw him coming and prepared

for battle. When he came within two feet of the nest they pounced upon him. They stung him on the neck and nose and cheeks and arms. Trying to beat them off, Tieg lost his grip on the branch and fell.

He had the bad judgment to fall on the honey badger, which promptly bit him on the leg. This animal is a ferocious fighter and will take on an opponent a dozen times its own size. It proceeded to rip holes in Tieg's clothes with its sharp claws. Tieg shook it off and ran.

He stopped when he found that the ratel was not following. Instead, the animal was climbing up to the bees' nest.

Tieg felt as happy about it as if he had planned it that way. What could be better? The ratel would do the work and he, Tieg, would get the honey. It occurred to him that he was pretty smart, after all.

The bees swarmed around the ratel but their stings did not disturb him in the least. His tough hide was like a coat of armour. He clawed the nest from the branch and it fell to the ground. The bees still buzzed around the branch that had been their home.

This was easy picking. All that Tieg needed to do was to take the big honeycomb, treat himself, then carry all the rest to the village, give everybody a little of it, and allow everyone to think what a clever fellow he really was.

But the honey badger was clawing open the comb and eating the sweet contents. The bird fluttered about constantly, waiting its turn. Tieg also waited. His heart sank when he saw that the ratel was tearing the honeycomb to bits. There would be nothing much left to take to the village.

Finally the ratel stopped eating and looked up at the bird as if to say, 'Now it's your turn'. He ambled off, full of honey and quite content. He had left enough for his flying friend.

The bird promptly sailed in to get its own dinner but was as promptly scared away by Tieg. What could he do now? He wasn't going to eat after an animal. Besides, what was left, though satisfactory to a bird, was so crumbled and mixed with dirt that no man would want to eat it.

Tieg was angry. Angry with the honey badger, and angry with the honey bird which had led him here on a fool's errand. Instead of allowing the bird to enjoy its dinner in peace, he fiercely ground every bit of honeycomb deep into the dirt, then, quite proud of himself, stood off to see what the bird would make of it.

The honey guide flew down and pecked about but

found nothing. It flew up to perch on a branch and peer at Tieg with one eye. For a while it was quite silent. Tieg was highly pleased with himself. It was a pleasure to be able to cheat somebody or something, even if it was only a bird.

Presently the honey guide stirred. It fluttered a bit and found its voice. It took off and flew to another tree, *cherping* loudly and fluttering excitedly.

So this was another come-on, Tieg thought. The bird would lead him to another beehive. This time there would be no honey badger to make a mess of things.

He followed the bird, which flew from tree to tree, finally stopping at a hollow stump and circling about it just as it had circled around the branch.

The hive must be in the stump. The trees cast heavy shade and Tieg could not see into the hollow, but he noticed that there were no bees flying about. That was good – perhaps they were away on an expedition, leaving the home unguarded. All he had to do this time was to reach in and take out the entire honeycomb, perfect and unbroken, and carry it off to the village.

He reached in and was immediately bitten by very sharp teeth. He pulled out his hand and whatever it was that had bitten him clung onto it.

Out came a cat-like animal spotted like a leopard, but smaller, with a black mask over its face.

It was no sooner out than it sprayed Tieg with a shower of evil-smelling secretion so strong that it might have paralysed a skunk. He swung it about trying to free his hand, but only succeeded in provoking it to send out more foul-smelling blasts that soaked him from head to toe.

It was the civet's method of self-defence. All animals, big and small, had learned to leave the civet alone. The smell was like that of very strong ammonia. It burned the inside of the nostrils of any creature that smelled it. Strangely enough, the stuff was used commercially as a base for perfumes. Of course its odour was completely changed in the process. But in its raw state there was nothing more disagreeable. If a monkey was sprayed, the other monkeys would have nothing to do with him. And, unluckily, the stink had a lasting quality and could not be washed away or rubbed off.

The civet prowls about at night but lies up during the day in some dark hole. The hollow stump was this animal's home sweet home, and it hotly resented being disturbed. After it had bitten deep and sprayed out everything it had to give, it dropped again into its hollow, giving some low-pitched, throaty coughs as if it could hardly stand its own smell.

11
The Salty Baboon

Searching for the leader of the gang that had slaughtered sixty gorillas, Hal and his men walked into the village of Kala.

It was a poor village. The houses were small and had no windows. The walls were of mud, the roofs were thatch made of papyrus – the same plant from which the ancient Egyptians made paper.

The people did not look too healthy but they were in a gay mood because this was the day when they would celebrate the election of a new chief. There would be a solemn ceremony when the present chief, now eighty years old, would pass on his authority to his son.

But this morning the old man was still chief, so Hal inquired the way to his house. He found a fine old gentleman with all the best qualities of a chief, but the withered body of a man who all his life had never had enough to eat.

After the usual courteous greetings spoken by Hal in English and translated into Swahili by Joro, Hal asked:

'Do you know a man named Nero? He hunts gorillas.'

'Yes, I know him.'

'Will he be here today?'

I hope not. He is not welcome in this village.'

'We hope he will come,' Hal said. 'We want to invite him to go with us to the police and explain why he is killing gorillas without a permit.'

'Good,' the chief said. 'He should be punished for killing our people.'

'Your people? The people of this village?'

'No. Our neighbours in the forest. The great tribes without speech.'

Hal was puzzled. Joro explained. 'He means the gorillas. Many villages do not believe that the gorillas are animals. They say that they are men who have lost the power of speech.'

Hal did not argue this point. He was satisfied to let the old chief believe whatever he chose to believe. He had to admit that the gorillas were better men than some men he knew.

'Don't you ever have trouble with these – tribes of the forest?' he asked.

'Never. If we leave them alone they never bother us.'

Hal looked out into the gardens surrounding the village. 'But I see some of them stealing your vegetables right now.'

'No, no,' the chief said. 'Those are not the forest people. Those are baboons. They are only animals. They trouble us very much. They steal our food and we go hungry. And now we have not only hunger but thirst.'

'But you have waterholes.'

'They have dried up,' the chief said sadly.

Hal tried to remember something he had read about the baboons and water. These animals didn't require much water. They usually got enough out of the green stuff that they ate. But they had the rare ability to detect the presence of water beneath the soil. If they became very thirsty they would locate water and dig down to it. But how make a baboon thirsty enough to want to dig?

'Do you have salt?' he asked.

'Salt we have. But it only makes us more thirsty.'

"Then it would make a baboon thirsty,' Hal explained. 'Perhaps thirsty enough to dig a well for you in your own garden. I'm not promising that it can be done. But would you like us to try?'

The old man nodded gravely but seemed to have little faith in the experiment. 'We thank you for your thought,' he said. 'It will do no harm to try.'

'We shall need a rope,' Hal said.

The chief sent one of his women for a line. She brought a rope that was not a rope. But it would do. It was one of the lianas that hang from the great trees.

Hal called together his men. 'Catch the biggest, strongest baboon you can get. Bring him here.'

The men, puzzling over this strange order, proceeded to the garden. The baboons did not run. Being the boldest of the primates, they kept on rooting out and devouring vegetables even when the men had closed round them.

In the meantime, one of the chief's women brought a large gourd filled with salt. It was not good clean commercial salt, for it had been scraped from a forest salt pan, but it was good enough for the purpose.

The baboon was brought. 'Now, lay it out,' Hal said,

'flat on its back – hold its arms and legs down – prise its jaws apart with that stick.'

The baboon struggled but the odds against it were too great. Hal began to force-feed it with salt. He felt a little guilty for doing this even to a baboon but after all, the animal should pay for damaging the gardens. Hal did not stop until the gourd was empty and the baboon was full.

'All right. Let him go.'

Perhaps any other animal would have made straight for the forest. The baboon only joined its companions, then turned and made faces at the men who had tormented it. How long it would take for the salt to do its work, Hal did not know. Perhaps the experiment would not work at all. The baboon sat sulking among the vegetables. With a stuffed stomach, he had no desire to eat more.

Hal waited and wondered. When the animal became thirsty he might wander off into the forest, perhaps many miles away, before he began to dig for water.

But Hal didn't think so. A baboon rarely goes off on its own. Besides, the ground in the forest would be full of roots and digging would be difficult if not impossible. In the garden the soil was soft, and clear of roots and stones.

It was nearly an hour before the baboon rose and began to explore. Then he walked about with his head down, using whatever mysterious senses elephants, rhinos, baboons and other animals employ to locate underground water.

Then he fixed upon a spot that suited him and began to dig. His great claw-like hands made excellent shovels. He soon had help. Baboons have a strong instinct for teamwork. In this respect they are quite different from some other animals, such as the hyena which is a loner, and seldom co-operates with other hyenas. If one baboon, especially a leader, starts a job the others will promptly join him.

So a dozen hands scooped away the dirt and the well rapidly deepened. They kept at it until at a depth of about twelve feet water began to ooze into the pit. It was muddy at first, but the salt-filled male did not wait for it to clear. He drank deeply.

The people of the village ran to get their calabashes and climbed down the sloping side of the well to capture the water that was now nearly two feet deep.

The old chief thanked Hal and the villagers looked at him as if he were some sort of magician.

There was only one thing wrong with that well. It

brought in other baboons from the forest. Soon there were twice as many baboons as before, enjoying the water and eating the growing vegetables. People beat gourds and pans to frighten them off, but baboons do not frighten easily. Instead, they nipped the legs of their tormentors with their strong, sharp teeth.

They even tore down a scarecrow that had been erected in the gardens to frighten them away. It had worked on most animals, but not baboons. The people looked again to Hal, the great magician. But the wizard had used up all his wizardry. He had no idea how to cope with this new situation.

Help was to come from an unexpected quarter. It was the great Andre Tieg who would step in at the right moment to save the gardens and save the day.

12
The Spotted Cat

The huge wooden drum of the village began to boom. It was time for the ceremony when the new chief would replace the old.

The people left the gardens and gathered in the open space at the centre of the village.

The aged chief made a long and beautiful speech that brought tears to the eyes of those who listened. They loved him and were sorry to have him step down. But when his son came before them they welcomed him as their new master with a great clatter of gourds and pans. He made a short and modest speech praising the work of his father over the years and promising to do everything in his power to carry on his father's work.

There was good reason for the shortness of his speech. He was interrupted by the arrival of Tieg.

Hal's men were disappointed to see that Tieg brought no honey. As for the villagers, they were amazed by the appearance of this huge fellow with his bristling yellow moustache, his cockatoo hair and his glass eye.

But most of all they were conscious of a penetrating

odour that seemed to burn the inside of their nostrils and start a fire in their heads. Those nearest to Tieg realized that the stench came from the big man's tattered and stained clothing. They shrank away from him as if he had the plague. They held their noses – but they must breathe, and when they did they were almost suffocated by the evil smell.

They looked to Hal for help, but Hal was helpless. They turned to their new chief. Here was his first problem as headman of the village. Here was a test case. He must do something. If he succeeded he would be respected. If he failed he would start his rule with a black mark against him. Another even more serious problem confronted him – the problem of what to do to save the gardens from the baboons.

The young chief, urged on by his people, approached Tieg. But when he came within ten feet of him he stopped. It was as if he had come up against a stone wall – an invisible wall of smell so sickening that he could not go further. He looked around helplessly. He knew he was making a poor spectacle of himself as leader of his village.

'I wish we could do something for him,' Hal said.

'I think I can,' said Roger.

Hal was amused by his young brother's courage. 'Well, if you can, go to it.'

Roger called Joro. 'I want to speak to the chief – privately – in his own house. Will you interpret?'

Joro smiled and nodded. He did not think it strange for this fourteen-year-old boy to expect a private conference with a village chief. Roger had already won the respect of the crew by his single-handed capture of the gorilla and the white python.

Joro introduced Roger to the chief, who looked at him curiously and a little impatiently because he did not care to be bothered by a boy when there were important matters waiting for his attention. He reluctantly consented and the three entered his house and closed the door.

'Now, what is it?' demanded the young headman. 'I can't give you much time.'

Some fifteen minutes later they emerged from the house, the chief carrying a blanket. He came within ten feet of Tieg and threw the blanket at his feet.

'You will remove your clothes,' he ordered. 'You will wear this instead.'

Tieg glared at him. 'I will do no such thing.'

Hal said, 'Mr Tieg, please do as he says.'

Sulkily, Tieg drew the blanket around himself and slipped off his rags beneath it.

'Now,' said the new chief, 'you will carry your clothes out and put them on that scarecrow.'

Tieg threaded his way through the crowd of feeding baboons and the people followed to watch him clothe the figure in the field.

Immediately there was a commotion among the baboons. They stopped feeding and began to give signals of acute distress. Their sense of smell, more acute than man's, was all the more tortured by this frightful stink that the civet used so effectively against all enemies from baboon to elephant.

Chattering angrily, the baboons made off into the forest.

The villagers roared with laughter and relief. Their new chief was pretty smart, after all.

'Where did you pick up this smell?' Roger asked Tieg. Tieg described the spot, the hollow stump, and the odoriferous cat.

'Yes, yes,' said the headman. 'I know the place. And I know the ways of the spotted cat. The smell will not last for ever. When it is gone we can go back to the spotted cat for more.'

The people were dancing in honour of their new chief, young in years, old in wisdom. The village medicine man led them in a chant praising their new leader who on his very first day rid them of the baboons that had troubled them for years. Truly, a great man.

Roger was satisfied to leave it that way. He didn't want the credit. Not that he didn't like credit, but he thought it must be tough for a young fellow to take over the control of a village after it had been so well ruled for many years by his father. At such a moment the new man needed all the credit he could get.

But how about Nero, the man whose gang had that day killed sixty gorillas in order to steal their babies?

Hal expressed his disappointment that the fellow had not shown up. 'I'd like to have told him what I think of him,' he said to the ex-chief.

'He was here,' the old man said. 'But when he saw you he went away.'

'Why didn't you tell me he was here?'

'Because I didn't want any fighting on this day when my son became chief.'

Hal could understand that. 'Perhaps you were right,' he said. 'But I'll get him yet.'

'Unless he gets you first,' said the old man. 'He won't

hesitate to do to you what he did to our sixty friends in the forest. Watch out for him.'

Upon returning to camp, the first order of business was to feed Lady Luck, Snow White and the two babies.

The youngsters still clung to Roger's shoulders.

'There's a cage about the right size for them on that Powerwagon,' Hal said.

But when the two little orphans were put into the cage they immediately began to wail.

'They want their mother,' Hal said. 'And that's you.'

'You mean to imply that I'm an ape?' Roger said.

Hal looked him over carefully. 'Well, you don't look like one to me, but you can't fool the babies. They know a gorilla when they see one.'

Roger laughed. 'That's all right. I don't mind being a gorilla. They have better manners than some people I know.'

He went back to the cage and opened it. At once the two youngsters scrambled out and climbed up to his shoulders. Their wails died down to little whimpers. 'We'll take them into the room with us,' Roger announced.

'Our room is no zoo,' objected Hal.

'It will be, with four gorillas in it.'

'Four?'

'Of course. You say I'm an ape – and you're my brother, aren't you?'

The four apes entered the cabin. The two little ones were shivering a bit from the cold of late afternoon. Roger tucked them into his own bed. They clutched the pillow just as they had clutched his shoulders. They were forlorn little things and must have something to hang on to.

'Gorillas love fruit,' Roger said. 'I'll get some out of the supply truck.'

Hal stopped him. 'I don't think they're old enough for it. It would give them colic and perhaps dysentery. When they're a little older they can eat mashed bananas, bamboo shoots, wild celery and such.'

'But they can't wait until they get older. What do they eat now?'

'Perhaps Pablum and wheatgerm. Even that might upset them. What they really need first is mother's milk. Since they've adopted you as their mother, it's up to you to nurse them.'

'And you think I can't? Wait a minute.'

Roger left the room. He walked over to the cage containing Snow White and Lady Luck. He spoke to Lady Luck, the gorilla, in low quiet tones. She snarled at him, slapping the floor of the cage with her hands.

For half an hour he stood there in the growing cold, talking to her. Then he ventured to put his hand between the bars, but made no attempt to touch her. She drew back from the hand, smelling it suspiciously. After some minutes he moved his hand directly in front of her face.

Suddenly her jaws opened and her great teeth closed on the hand. Roger controlled his desire to pull it free. He let it lie between the sharp teeth and continued speaking, quietly. The jaws did not tighten on the hand.

Some of the men had gathered to watch this peculiar performance. They had watched Roger work with animals before this, and had no fear that he would be hurt. All the same, they stood ready to help him if he needed help.

Lady Luck's jaw relaxed. Roger slowly withdrew his hand but left it directly in front of those great teeth where it could be seized again if the gorilla so wished.

After a few minutes he slowly extended his hands towards the gorilla's neck. She seemed to take no notice. He caressed the back of the head and the neck. The lady wouldn't admit that she liked it, but she plainly did not dislike it.

He went around to the cage door. He told the men, 'Stand by, in case she tries to escape.' He opened the door, went in, closed the door.

The gorilla stood up to her full height and slapped herself with her cupped hands, warning this intruder to behave himself. But it was a very poor show of anger. Plainly, she was not really angry, but only a little nervous.

Snow White, the python, was coiled in the corner. Roger stepped lightly to avoid disturbing her. He opened the door and stood in the opening. When Lady Luck moved towards the door, he did not try to stop her, but stepped aside to let her pass. She hesitated. He took her great hairy paw that could have laid him flat with one blow, and led her out, closing the door behind him. The men circled around him, but did not come too close.

He led the lady to his door and through it into the room, then closed the door.

Hal lay on his bed, half asleep. He woke with a start and sat up to stare into the great black face of a gorilla not three inches from his own. At first he thought he was dreaming and this was his brother who had really turned into an ape. Then he scrambled out of bed and retreated to the far side of the room.

'Don't be afraid,' Roger said. 'She's a perfect lady. And I'm hoping she's a good mother.'

The gorilla noticed the two little fragments of apedom in the bed. She ambled over to get a closer look. They gazed up at her with eager, hungry eyes.

Would it work? Both Hal and Roger knew that grown-up gorillas loved all gorilla babies whether they are their own or not. In fact the real mother often has trouble keeping away the aunts, uncles and friends who want to pet her infant. Roger was depending upon this fact of gorilla nature.

He was not mistaken. The babies were already scrambling up into the arms of their foster mother. She gathered them close in her hairy embrace. Presently there was a suckling sound. The babies had found their milk. The feeding problem was solved.

Hal looked on, smiling. 'Well I'll be darned. Now you really have turned this room into a zoo.'

'Oh, I'm not quite done yet,' Roger said. 'I'm going to bring in Snow White too.'

'Not in here,' exclaimed Hal.

'Where else? She was nearly stolen last night. Whoever

or whatever chewed up that lock may be back tonight.'

'But doesn't it occur to you,' Hal said, 'that there's nothing a python would like better than to gobble up those two gorilla babies?'

'Gee, I hadn't thought of that,' Roger admitted. Here was a new problem. This time it was Hal who solved it.

13
The Balling Gun

Hal called Mali. He was the chief of the ten men who had stayed in camp during the day to guard the gorilla, Lady Luck, and the beautiful white python with the blue eyes, Snow White.

'Did you feed them?' Hal asked.

'We fed the gorilla,' Mali said.

'What did she eat?'

'Bananas, carrots, pineapple and bamboo shoots.'

'And how about the python?'

'She wouldn't take a thing. We offered her a warthog that we had just killed this morning. She wouldn't even look at it.'

'Perhaps she had eaten before we caught her.'

'I don't think so,' Mali said. 'If she had swallowed an animal there would be a bulge in her hide. But she's as slender as a dancing girl. Besides, if she had eaten, she would have been sleepy when we tried to take her. She wouldn't have fought the way she did.'

'You're right,' Hal said. 'Get enough men to help you and bring her in here.'

Mali's eyes widened. 'You don't mean here – in this room?'

'Yes, in this room. You've guarded her all day. I don't want you to have to guard her all night too. And she ought to eat. Bring me that warthog – and a balling gun.'

Hal was not surprised that the python had refused food. Any animal when captured may be so upset that it will not eat. Sometimes it is only a matter of hours, sometimes the fasting will go on for days until the creature dies of starvation.

Mali went out on his errand. It was half an hour before the door opened again to admit a strange procession. Snow White's darting tongue and blazing blue eyes came first, then Mali, firmly gripping the snake's neck so that the head could not turn and bite. Then came a parade of fourteen men, seven on each side of the snake, holding it tightly so that it could not coil.

Hal took Mali's place, and Mali went out to fetch the warthog and the balling gun.

The thing known as a balling gun is not a gun. It is an instrument used to force-feed an animal that refuses to eat. It consists of a long metal rod ending in a cup-shaped depression. You put a ball or chunk of food or medicine in the cup and push it so far back into the animal's throat that it must swallow it.

While the men firmly held the unwilling snake, the jaws were forced open and the cup in which the warthog had been placed was pushed far back into the throat. Snow White did her best to spew it out, but it was no use. The swallowing muscles went into action and down went the warthog into the creature's stomach. The balling gun was withdrawn.

The huge bulge in Snow White's midriff did not add to the snake's beauty.

'All right,' Hal said, 'let her go.'

The men laid the snake on the floor and stood off, half expecting her to attack. But nothing was farther from her mind. All she wanted to do now was to go to sleep.

How long would she sleep? That would depend upon how long it took to digest her meal. It might be a matter of days, or weeks. After a very large feeding, snakes have been known to lie dormant for several months.

One thing was certain. The two baby gorillas were perfectly safe in the same room with the great snake that usually had an excellent appetite for baby gorillas.

*

The door was locked and all the members of the 'zoo' including Snow White, Lady Luck, the two baby gorillas and the two humans were safe for the night. Or so it seemed.

Lady Luck was content to sleep on the floor. 'Her long hair will keep her warm,' Roger guessed.

'Probably,' Hal said. 'But just to make sure I'll give her one of my blankets.'

He laid it over her, and the way she snuggled into it showed that she appreciated it.

Roger crawled in between the two infant gorillas. At first they sleepily protested. But when they discovered that what was between them gave off a pleasant heat they wedged themselves as close to it as possible. They frequently wriggled to get into a better position, and talked in their sleep. Roger was going to have a rather uneasy night.

He envied Hal who had a whole bed to himself. Hal went blissfully to sleep but woke with a start an hour later when he felt a cold something sharing the bed with him. Now he too had a sleeping partner. Snow White had crept in under the blankets.

Unlike other animals, a snake has no heating system of its own. It takes on the temperature of the surrounding air. Even though Mount Mikeno is near the equator, the night air is chill at an altitude of ten thousand feet. Ordinarily the snake would be spending the night deep in its hole where some of the warmth of the day still remained. Lacking a hole, it would crawl under heavy brush.

Lacking both hole and brush, Snow White sensibly crept under Hal's covers. However, there was one good thing about her. She didn't wriggle and she didn't talk. Slowly digesting her warthog dinner, she could be trusted to be a silent partner in Hal's bed.

So Hal thought. He was a little disturbed when he woke later to find that the snake had thrown a coil of her body over his own.

What should he do about this? If she chose to constrict, she could squeeze the breath out of him and he would die in a few minutes. Should he struggle to free himself? That would excite the snake and make matters worse.

He tried to look at it from Snow White's point of view. She couldn't have done this with any idea of attacking him. He was too big to swallow. In fact, she had no appetite. It had been necessary to force-feed her. She would certainly want nothing more until her present load was digested.

THE BALLING GUN

By the slight moon-glow that came in through the window he could see her head on the pillow beside his. This gave him a moment of panic. He controlled himself with difficulty. There was no danger. Her great jaws were closed. All that he needed to do was to keep quiet. He must not even call Roger – that might awake and excite her.

There could be only one reason why she had wrapped herself around him. He was something warm.

But in spite of all his experience with animals he couldn't help being a little nervous in this situation. He knew he wouldn't sleep another wink that night. But he was young and had had an active day. In five minutes he was as sound asleep as the python.

14
Fire

When the screams of elephants broke the night silence, the first to be disturbed by the noise was the creature without ears. Snow White felt the sound waves in her hundreds of nerve-ends. Frightened, she slid out of Hal's bed and retreated to the farthest corner of the room.

Only a hard pounding on the door woke the other occupants of the Hunt zoo. Hal recognized Joro's voice.

'Fire, bwana, fire!'

The boys tumbled out. Their end of the cabin was ablaze. The dried-out boards of the cabin wall burned fiercely.

The men were already bringing buckets of water from the lake and dousing the flames. But there weren't enough buckets for thirty men.

The fire seemed to light the whole sky. That was strange. This blaze alone couldn't give out so much light. Then Hal saw the reason.

'Look, the volcano!'

Ten miles away to the south-east, Nyiragongo volcano was in full eruption, spitting out rivers of red-hot lava and throwing aloft a column of fire a mile or more high. The wind was blowing towards the cabin. Had it carried sparks that had started the cabin fire?

Hal's first thought was of the animals – Snow White, Lady Luck and the two small gorillas. Would they be burned alive? He flung the door open to let them escape. With sinking heart, he looked for the loss of the valuable animals he had worked so hard to obtain.

But the animals did not come out. Terrified by the fire, they felt safer in the dark room than in the blazing light outside.

How to get them out? It would be easy to remove the babies, but it would require many men to bring out the powerful female gorilla and the great snake. And the men were busy fighting the fire. Those who had no buckets were trying to suffocate the flames with blankets and canvas.

Help came from an unexpected quarter. The elephants became firemen. There were three of them and they had formed the habit of coming every night to visit the lake and roam around the cabin. They would stand near the campfire and enjoy its warmth. The men had made friends of them, feeding them bamboo shoots, stalks of sugar cane and wild celery.

Now the elephants paid back all they owed. With an intelligence matched in the animal world only by the great apes and the dolphin, they repeated a performance reported many years ago by the man who was buried here, Carl Akeley, in his book *In Brightest Africa*. He observed the ability of an elephant to put out a fire by shooting a stream of water from his trunk.

The great beasts heartily dislike grass fires and have checked many in this way. If they had not been checked they would have become forest fires and elephants could have done nothing to stop them.

All this flashed through Hal's mind as he saw the great animals fill their huge fire hoses with water at the lake and then trundle over to quench the blaze. Every trunkful was equal to a dozen or more bucketfuls. Another half hour of hard work and nothing was left of the fire except a few plumes of smoke from the wet boards.

Now that the danger was past the precious animals might escape. Hal hastily closed the door of his bedroom menagerie.

The elephants were still drawing water, but only to

toss over themselves to wash cinders and ashes from their hides. At a suggestion from Roger the men took them two large hands of bananas as a reward for their fire-fighting services.

Hal was talking to Joro. 'What do you think started that fire? Sparks from the volcano?'

Before Joro could answer, Tieg, who was standing by, said, 'Of course. What else?'

Joro looked at him doubtfully. Then he looked up at the volcano smoke passing overhead. 'I suppose hot cinders from the volcano could be blown ten miles,' he said. 'But it doesn't seem very likely.'

'Likely or not, that's what happened,' Tieg asserted. He trudged off to his room to catch up on sleep. Joro's eyes followed him.

'Perhaps. Perhaps not.'

'You have some other explanation?' Hal asked.

'Maybe. We were sleeping in the shed. The camp-fire was outside in the open place. I was half awake. It seemed to me I saw someone take a burning stick from the fire and walk away. I didn't think much about it. A few of the men sometimes get up during the night and get fire to make coffee.'

'You couldn't see who it was?'

'No. The smoke almost hid him. It was more like a black shadow than a man.'

'How large was – this thing?'

'Big.'

'As big as – Tieg?'

'Yes. As big as Tieg. Or as big as the gorilla with the bullet in him. You call him Gog. But of course it couldn't have been the gorilla. He wouldn't have been that smart.'

Hal was not so sure. 'I don't know,' he said. 'Apes are very imitative. He may have seen one of the men take a brand from the fire. I'm sure he's been watching the camp, waiting for a chance to get back at us because he thinks we murdered his family. And he must be a pretty angry beast with that bullet wound driving him half crazy with pain. I wish we could catch him and get the bullet out of him. But that fire – there's one other rascal who might have started it.'

'You don't mean one of our own men?'

'No, no. I mean the man we didn't see yesterday. But we've seen his handiwork – those sixty dead gorillas. Nero can guess that we are going to report him to the commandant. And that's exactly what we'll do this morning.'

His words were almost drowned out by the roar of thunder over the volcano. Fork lightning played around the burning mountain. This was no ordinary thunderstorm. Not a drop of rain was falling. The thunder and lightning were caused by the high electric tension produced in the air by the eruption.

Suddenly Hal and Joro were bathed in purple flame. Their bodies gave off sparks. There was a crackling and fizzing noise, as if they were being burned alive. Purple flashes leaped from the tip of Hal's nose, his ears, his fingers and toes. Joro put on an equally fine display. Their heads were surrounded by flashing purple crowns. Still neither of them felt any electric shock.

'Even the god of the volcano is against us,' Joro said.

Hal laughed. 'It won't hurt you. It's St Elmo's fire.'

'What's that?'

'An electric discharge caused by the fight between the heat rising from the volcano and the cold air around it. It disturbs all the air within a radius of twenty miles or so of a volcano.'

'Well,' Joro said, 'I hope it scares Tieg or Gog or Nero or anybody else who is sneaking around trying to make trouble.'

Perhaps it did just that, for there was no more sign

of an enemy that night. Hal and Roger tried to get back to sleep, but it is not easy to fall asleep while sparkling with purple fire and sizzling like a fire-cracker. The room was half lit by a purple glow and Snow White's nervous tongue darted purple flame. Meanwhile the brilliant lightning and terrific blasts of thunder promised rain that never came.

Something was raining down but it was not rain. Breakfast, eaten outside as usual, was liberally sprinkled with falling ashes.

There seemed to be two sunrises, one east, one west. On one side was the rising sun, on the other the blaze of the volcano.

Smoke rose from the forest in a dozen places where cinders had started brush fires. Any one of them might find its way to the camp and finish what the night fire had begun. And this morning there was no fire brigade of elephants to help protect the cabin.

It was a good day to stay at home. So Joro was surprised when Hal said, 'Leave half of the men here to take care of the camp. We'll take the others with us.'

'Where are we going, bwana?' Joro asked.

'To Rumangabo, to see the commandant. We've got to report what Nero is doing to the gorillas.'

'But Nero must guess that you are going to report him. He and his gang will be waiting for you somewhere along the road.'

'I know it,' Hal said. 'That's why I want to take along fifteen good men.'

Joro studied the volcano. A river of boiling lava flowed down the east slope. 'The road that we'll have to take is right there at the foot of the mountain. Probably it's already blocked by that flow.'

'That's a chance we'll have to take,' Hal said. 'There's another reason why I want to go right now. There must be animals trapped by the streams of lava. Perhaps we can rescue some of them. Otherwise they'll be burned alive.'

15
The Crater

In a Land-Rover and Powerwagon, Hal and Roger with fifteen of their men set out on their dangerous mission.

The dirt road dropped steeply to the village of Kibumba at the foot of Mikeno, then turned left to hug the base of flaming Nyiragongo, Why come so perilously close? There is no network of roads in Africa like those in Europe or America. You go where you must, not where you will. There was no other way to Rumangabo.

They sweated in the heat of the burning mountain. The boiling lava had set fire to the forest. It was a thrilling sight – the blazing mountain two miles high and, spouting from the top of it, another mile of fire carrying up rocks which then fell and tore their way through the burning forest. There was the double thunder, in the sky three miles up and in the volcano itself.

They were so dazzled by the mountain that they failed to watch the road. Suddenly they found themselves crossing a lava river. Fortunately it had cooled a little and turned black. It still sent up great volumes of steam.

Some of the men yelled 'Stop!' But Joro, at the wheel of the first car, believed that their only hope was in speed. He could not tell whether the lava was soft or hard. The wheels might sink into it and be glued fast. He would not allow time for that to happen. An instant too long, and the terrific heat that still remained in the lava would blow out the tyres. He shot across as a skater skims over thin ice.

He looked back and was glad to see that the other car was coming just as fast. But there was a third vehicle, a truck full of men, evidently Nero and his gang. The white man himself was at the wheel. His nerve failed him, and he stepped hard on the brake. Perhaps he hoped to stop short of the lava, but the momentum of the heavy truck carried it into the middle of the steaming stream. There it stopped, the wheels sank in, and nothing short of a charge of dynamite would ever tear that truck loose from the clutch of congealing lava.

Hal clapped Joro on the back. 'Good boy!' he cried. 'That will give them time to think things over.'

Joro grinned, but did not accept Hal's praise. 'Only trouble is,' he said, 'they'll be there when we come back.'

It was all downhill now to the north end of one of the most beautiful lakes in Africa, Lake Kivu. No wonder they called this the African Riviera. The shore was a carpet of brilliant flowers, and magnificent crested cranes strutted about among the strangest of strange trees, the euphorbia or candelabra, looking like gigantic candle holders thirty feet high.

Now they turned west through the Mitumba Mountains to Rumangabo.

Here they were welcomed by the commandant who had given them their hunting permit.

'I hope your work is going well,' he said.

'A little slowly at first,' Hal said. 'But we have a large female gorilla, two small gorillas, and a white python.'

The commandant's eyebrows went up.

'A white python? An albino, I presume.'

'No, a natural white.'

'Remarkable. I should say you have been very fortunate. I've heard of only one other white, and that was killed by locals. Yours will be protected in the zoo. Protection is our greatest problem. That is why we are very careful about issuing permits.'

'That's what I came to see you about,' Hal said. 'Did you issue a permit to a man named J. J. Nero?'

The commandant looked through his register. 'No such name here.'

'Well, the name is here,' Hal said, passing over the notebook opened at the page bearing the signature, J. J. Nero.

The commandant thumbed through the notebook, reading the records of animals killed, animals taken and animals shipped.

'Why, this fellow's doing a land office business. How did you come by this book?'

'We found it among the dead bodies of sixty adult gorillas that had been slaughtered in order to get their babies.'

'Did you say sixty? You mean six?'

'I mean sixty. We made a careful count.'

'That is mass murder. We'll send out a patrol at once and try to round up Nero and his gang. But we lack men. Therefore I deputize you to help us.'

'We'll do what we can,' Hal assured him. He was about to go out the door when the commandant said, 'By the way, how about Tieg? I hope he's not giving you trouble.' Hal shook his head, but did not answer. 'You remember,' added the commandant, 'I didn't recommend him.'

'That's right, you didn't,' Hal said. He wanted

to avoid saying anything against poor, blundering, troublesome Tieg. 'We chose to take him on. So he's our responsibility.'

Now with power to arrest Nero, if he could find him, Hal took his party back to the flaming mountain.

There was the truck, deep in lava. But Nero and his men had disappeared.

'Well,' Hal said, 'we can't go hunting for them just now. We've got to see if any animals have been trapped by the eruption.'

They climbed the mountain – through the strange heather trees and twenty-foot tree ferns, the groves of bamboo, the whistling thorn trees, the monarchs of the forest two hundred feet tall trailing tough lianas, the nettles shoulder-high bristling with barbs that penetrate heavy clothing and have been known to kill horses, the musanga trees that looked like huge umbrellas.

They must avoid the rivers of lava and the forest fires the lava had started. A small animal escaping from the fire was caught by Roger.

'What is it?' he asked.

'A bush-baby,' Hal said. 'It's a cousin of the monkeys.

Pretty little thing. Makes a good pet.'

It was only the size of a small squirrel, had large eyes and ears, soft woolly fur and a long tail.

'They live in the trees,' Hal said, 'and like to sleep all day. But this little fellow had no chance today. He's really like a very tiny kangaroo. He walks on his hind legs and sits up as straight as you do. I hope he appreciates his good luck – meeting you just when he needed you most.'

Certainly the little jumper made no attempt to leap from Roger's hands. Instead he cowered close to the boy's bush jacket, trembling as his big round eyes gazed at the forest fire and the golden river.

Roger slipped it into a pocket of his jacket. Only its head was in the open. It gradually stopped shaking, then withdrew its head and curled up to do what it did best in the daytime. It slept.

'Not very lively,' Roger complained.

Hal laughed. 'It will be lively enough when it gets dark,' he said. 'You'll be lucky if you get any sleep tonight. It's as full of fun at night as it is full of sleep in the daytime. It almost flies. It will be leaping clear across the room. With those big eyes it can see very well in the dark.'

'What does it eat?'

'Anything you eat and some things you don't – fruits, leaves, insects and even spider's webs. Have you ever eaten a spider's web? Delicious. At least, the bush-baby thinks so.'

A little later, Roger collected a playmate for his bush-baby. If the bush-baby looked like a tiny kangaroo, its playmate looked like a miniature edition of an elephant. It actually had a trunk which it usually held upright but could move about in any direction. The whole animal was less than half the size of the bush baby.

'What you have there is unique,' Hal said. 'An elephant shrew. It's the smallest of all the mammals.'

'But it looks so much like the biggest,' Roger said.

'That's Nature's joke,' Hal suggested, 'to make the largest land mammal on earth and the smallest in the same style. It ought to be good company for the bush-baby since they both sleep by day and are lively at night.'

'But it's not like the elephant in one way,' Roger said. 'It can't defend itself.'

'Yes it can. Handle it gently or you'll find out what it can do. See that little gland on the side of its body? If it doesn't like you it can spurt out a fluid that would make a skunk hold its nose.'

Roger very carefully slipped the two-inch-long 'elephant' into his other pocket.

'Be careful not to bump that pocket against a tree,' Hal advised, 'or you'll smell as bad as Tieg after he disturbed the civet. But if it's gently treated it will behave perfectly.'

Roger put his hand in his pocket and stroked the tiny creature. It was as small and soft as a new-born kitten.

'I don't suppose either of them is really worth anything,' he said.

'You'd be surprised. You're carrying a hundred dollars in each pocket. Anybody can have a pup or a kitten, but pets like these are very unusual and valuable. Dad will see that they get good homes.'

They climbed out of the forest and up a slope of cinders to stand on the edge of the crater. The volcano was resting but might explode again at any moment. Deep in the crater was a boiling lake the colour of an orange, for this was one of the few active volcanoes in the world to contain a lake of molten lava. Great bubbles the size of a house swelled up and burst to let out a cloud of steam. There was a constant grinding sound as partly hardened masses of lava were tossed about like pebbles. 'I'm hot in front and cold behind,' Roger said. The heat from the boiling lake struck his face, and the wind, always cold at this altitude of two miles, chilled his back.

The view from this perch in the sky was magnificent. To the north a twin volcano, always active but not now in violent eruption, sent up a pillar of smoke. In every direction were dormant volcanoes, except to the south where lovely Lake Kivu stretched away like a great mirror.

Joro joined them. He did not bother about the view but seemed fascinated by the boiling lake. 'It's a terrible place,' he said. 'The people say that the ghosts of the dead live down there. They stir the fires and the fires send up death. No one can see it or feel it, nor smell it, but it makes a man sleepy and he closes his eyes, his breath stops, his spirit goes to join the ghosts. Not even the medicine men can explain it. It is some kind of witchcraft.'

'Sounds to me like carbon monoxide,' Hal said.

'What is that?'

'A poison gas. The same gas that comes from the exhaust pipe of a car. On the road, the breeze thins it or blows it away. But in any deep hole like this crater it becomes very strong and a man who breathes it may die without knowing that he is dying.'

'Look,' Roger exclaimed. 'What's that down there? Something moving. It's trying to get up, and can't.'

'Let's go down and see,' Hal said.

'But how about the gas?'

'It won't bother us if we make a quick trip.'

They clambered down the inside slope of the crater and the men followed. It was not more than three hundred feet to the moving thing. Now they could see that it was a female gorilla. But what was that in its arms? A baby gorilla with its eyes closed.

'It must be dead,' Hal guessed. The mother was struggling to climb out of the crater but would not give up the baby.

'Why do you suppose they came down here?' Roger wondered.

'They wouldn't do it of their own free will,' Hal said. 'They must have been trying to get away from somebody or something.'

The men closed around the faithful mother and her dead infant. They tried to catch her and carry her up the slope. When they almost had her, she fell and lay still. Hal felt her pulse. She was dead.

'There's nothing we can do here,' Hal said. He felt sure he was beginning to weaken. The deadly gas was doing its work. 'Let's get out of here – fast.'

A crashing sound above him made him look up. A rock the size of a ten-ton truck that had been poised on the edge of the crater was thundering down upon them. The men tried desperately to get out of its way, but one was caught and badly hurt. Carrying the injured man, the others climbed slowly to the top.

Joro examined the spot where the rock had rested. 'See those prints in the cinders? Men have been here. That rock didn't just fall – it was pushed.'

'We'll follow them,' Hal said. 'But first we'll do what we can for this fellow.'

The man was unconscious from shock. He was bruised and bloody and there were some broken bones. Without a first-aid kit, Hal did what he could. It was half an hour before the man regained consciousness. He got up and tried to walk, but fell again and had to be carried.

'Now let's see where these tracks lead,' Hal said. 'Joro, that's your job. Sorry they didn't wait to face us. Perhaps they're hiding somewhere, waiting to ambush us as we go down.'

16
Take 'em Alive

Hal was soon proved right – and wrong.

Nero and his gang were waiting in ambush, but they had picked a poor hideout. They had chosen a pit some twenty feet deep, masked by trees. It would have been perfect if it had not been for their most deadly enemy, carbon monoxide.

The gas, carried up by the force of the eruption, was heavier than air and therefore had settled down into any windless depressions such as this very pit. Nero and his men, huddled at the bottom of the pit, were now quite incapable of ambushing anybody. Unaware of the reason for the drowsiness, they had breathed the poison gas until they had been overcome by sleep – a sleep that would be permanent unless they were rescued at once.

'Pull them out,' Hal ordered.

His men, who usually obeyed him with alacrity, were slow to act. Mali said, 'Bwana, these are your enemies. They tried to kill you with that rock. They are out to murder you and your brother. Now they are passing out, and nobody can blame you if you let them go.'

Hal disagreed. 'There's just one man here who is our enemy. That's Nero. We'll arrest him. I think the others are neither enemies nor friends. They simply take his orders. Pull them out, and be quick about it.'

Hal himself went down to haul out the white man. Nero was as limp as a jellyfish. He was too far gone to realize what was happening, but his heart was still beating and Hal was sure he would revive. All the Africans were removed from the deadly pit and laid out on the grass above where fresh air could sweep over them and chase out the poison gas from their lungs.

Their spears and bush knives were collected. Hal took Nero's revolver.

'Shall we tie them up?' Joro asked.

'No. Except Nero. Get a liana and tie his hands behind his back.'

Hal had a chance to study the gorilla killer. Nero was about his own height, a little over six feet, but quite a bit heavier. He had a peculiarly sour expression, as if he were having a bad dream. His mouth was drawn down at the corners and his cheeks were covered with black stubble.

'He's an ugly brute,' Roger commented.

'Ugly, but no brute,' Hal said. 'A brute is an animal,

and I don't know any animal that looks quite that unpleasant.'

In a quarter of an hour the gas victims began to revive. They remembered hiding in the pit and were surprised to find themselves lying on the grass above and surrounded by strangers. Their weapons were gone, and their leader was still unconscious.

'How did we get here?' one of them inquired.

'We pulled you out, stupid,' Mali told him. 'You were bewitched. You would have died.'

'You are the stupid ones,' the man answered. 'We know you. You are the men who follow the two young whites who are after gorillas. We are out to get you. You are stupid to give us another chance.'

'I think so too,' Mali said. 'So if you prefer I'll run you through with a spear right now.'

'You talk big,' the man replied. 'Our boss is stronger than your boys.'

'Is that so? There's your boss. Half-dead, no gun, hands tied. He will go to gaol.'

The gas victims sat up, rubbing their eyes, trying to realize what had happened.

Hal asked one of them, 'Why were you killing gorillas? Have they ever done you any harm?'

'Never.'

'Then why kill them?'

'We were paid.'

'You will be paid no longer.'

'If we are not paid, we will not work.'

'Now you are talking sense,' Hal said. 'Go back to your villages and live in peace.'

The men struggled to their feet and shambled off down the mountain without even a backward glance at Nero, whom they had obeyed only because he paid.

Hal shook Nero. The big fellow groaned, then opened his eyes. He looked about. 'Where am I?' he said dizzily. 'Where are my men? What's been going on?'

'Your men are taking a long walk,' Hal said. 'But you're a lucky fellow. You are going to ride.'

Mali and Toto pulled him to his feet and marched him down the mountain.

He tried to throw them off. 'Get your dirty hands off me.'

'Mind your manners,' Hal said. 'They are better men than you are.'

'You're not gonna get away with this, you know. You have no authority.'

'I happen to be deputized to arrest you,' Hal said.

The route they had followed up the mountain was now a river of lava. They had to find another way down.

The rain of red-hot stones began again. It was necessary to keep a sharp look-out above and dodge at the last moment.

They were so occupied in watching the sky that they almost failed to notice a large chimpanzee walking down the mountain hand in hand with the most beautiful monkey they had ever seen. It had evidently been struck by one of the falling rocks. It limped painfully and surely would have fallen if it had not been supported by the friendly chimp.

'It's a colobus,' Hal said. 'Prettiest of all monkeys. Lives in the tops of the tallest trees. But with the trees on fire, it had to come down. Isn't it a beauty? What's the chimp trying to say to us?'

The chimpanzee had stopped and was looking from one boy to the other, chattering loudly.

'Wish I understood chimp language,' Hal said. 'But I think he's asking us to help his disabled friend.'

He picked up the colobus. It did not struggle to escape. On the contrary, it was terrified by the fires and clung tightly to Hal's bush jacket.

'You've just seen two miracles,' Hal said. 'A chimp

157

helping a monkey: they usually have nothing to do with each other. And one of the wildest monkeys making friends with a man. The colobus generally stays as far away from men as it can get. It just shows what common danger will do. We're three very different animals – chimp, monkey and man – but we're all afraid of fire.'

They picked their way on down through the hot stones and streams of lava. The chimp kept close to them.

'That chimp sure was a Good Samaritan to help the monkey,' Roger said. 'If he stays with us I'm going to call him that.'

'Call him what?'

'Good Samaritan. Sam for short.'

'And what will you call this beauty?'

The colobus was half the size of the chimp, and the chimp was about half the size of a gorilla. But though the monkey was small in size he was large in dignity. Unlike the chimp, which had plenty to say, he was silent. His face was sad and serious. In fact he looked as sober as a judge. He had a great ruff of white whiskers that not only adorned his chin but covered his cheeks and even ran across his forehead. The hair on top of his head was black. So he looked like a little white-whiskered old man with a black skull-cap. His back was covered with glossy

jet-black fur. It glistened like spun glass. He had a white tuft on the end of his black tail.

But the most remarkable thing about him was his magnificent white robe. It covered his flanks and flowed down on both sides. He looked for all the world like a bishop.

'Bishop,' Roger exclaimed. 'That's what he is – a solemn little bishop.'

'Well,' Hal said, 'the bishop looks as if he were just about to celebrate mass, but the truth is he has been seen in very fine company. Colobus fur used to be extremely popular for trimming fashionable ladies' hats and coats.

While the fashion lasted two million colobus were destroyed. The fur is still used to make beautiful long-haired rugs in black and white, sometimes as many as twenty pelts in one rug. I hope that fashion will die too – if it doesn't, the colobus will soon be as extinct as the dodo.'

The bishop didn't seem to like this idea. He broke his silence to make a remark in a deep and solemn tone that contrasted oddly with the high-pitched chatter of the chimpanzee. 'He talks like a bishop too,' Roger said.

'Well, yes,' Hal agreed. 'But I am sorry to inform you, little brother, that he's quite unlike a bishop early in the morning. He starts the day with a fine whistling act and when he and your bush-baby put on a duet about an hour before you usually get up perhaps you'll be sorry you ever met them.'

Roger took his eyes off the ground long enough to stroke the soft-as-silk fur of the bishop. 'No, I won't be sorry.'

At the foot of the mountain they came upon a small lake. It was a lake of water, not lava, and yet it was boiling furiously. Evidently there were cracks in the lake floor that admitted volcanic gases at high temperature. It was like a tea-kettle on a very hot stove.

To escape the heat of the eruption, animals were taking refuge in the lake only to discover that it too was hot.

An animal came plunging through the brush in a see-sawing gallop. It plunged into the water. 'It's a kudu,' Hal said. 'They call it the rocking-horse – because of the way it rocks back and forth when it runs. Another rare animal. I wish we could get it.'

'If we don't get it right away it will be boiled to death,' said Roger. 'There's an old boat. Come on.'

They ran to the boat. Two rough poles served instead of paddles. They pushed out into the lake. It was an eerie experience, riding a sea of bubbles that burst to let out strong puffs of sulphur. The floorboards of the old punt were hot underfoot.

The 'rocking horse' seemed bewildered to find itself in hot water. It was too surprised to swim ashore. It appeared to be a poor swimmer.

'It's going to sink,' Roger exclaimed.

'No, it's blowing itself up. That's a special talent of the kudu.'

The animal was floating upside down, feet in the air. It was swelling up like a turkeycock. Now it was twice as large as when it entered the lake.

'Why does it do that?'

'To keep itself afloat. And it takes a lot of air to do that because it's a heavy beast, five hundred pounds or more. Grab one of its feet.'

Roger did so, and the 'rocking horse' kicked feebly. He allowed himself to be towed ashore. There, many hands were waiting to seize him by the horns and tail. One man tried to hold him down by straddling his back. The animal broke loose and set off with a rocking motion like that of a bucking horse. The man was tossed into a thorn bush and the kudu, wheezing out air like a punctured tyre, was again caught and steered by strong hands through the brush to the road and into a cage in the Powerwagon.

Some of the men who had remained near the lake were chasing another prize. This was a sitatunga, an antelope that walks on snowshoes – that is, its feet are so large and flat that it is quite at home walking on mud or marsh where a man would sink. At one side of the lake was a swamp and here the sitatunga sped over the surface while its pursuers went down in the gooey mass up to their chests.

Hal acted quickly. Taking other men with him, he ran around the marsh to meet the animal as it completed its crossing. It was caught by its long twisted horns and, after a bit of a struggle, 'Flatfoot' joined 'Rocking Horse' in the cage.

Here were two most unusual antelopes that would delight any circus or zoo fortunate enough to add them to its collection.

Hal felt the men should be rewarded. He called them together. 'Are you hungry?' They agreed with one voice. 'Come, Roger. We'll get them a fish dinner.' He leaped into the punt, and Roger followed.

'Just how do you expect to get fish without any line or net?'

Hal said, 'We were so busy bringing the kudu to shore you didn't notice that the fish are just waiting to be picked up.'

Under the bubbles great numbers of tilapia floated, belly up, perfectly cooked by the boiling lake. The boys flipped several dozen of them into the boat and pulled ashore. After all their exercise, climbing up and down the mountain, dodging hot stones, leaping over lava streams, wrangling animals, the men found the fish dinner delicious.

17
Bedroom Menagerie

The room was getting a bit crowded.

Besides two husky boys and the large female gorilla, Lady Luck – the python, Snow White – the two gorilla babies, there were four new guests: the elephant shrew, the bush-baby, the chimp who had won the title of Good Samaritan, Sam for short, and the white-robed colobus nicknamed The Little Bishop.

Roger had wanted to bring in also Rocking Horse and Flatfoot, the kudu and sitatunga. But Hal drew the line.

'They're too big,' Hal said. 'If they move in we'll have to move out.'

So they were housed in a cage on one of the catching cars.

Occupying another cage was the most dangerous animal of all – the gang leader and gorilla killer, J. J. Nero.

But he was just an overnight guest. In the morning Hal intended to deliver him to the commandant.

How would all the room-mates get along? Would the large ones destroy the little ones?

Lady Luck answered the question in her own way.

With the motherly instinct of the female gorilla, she at once cuddled the bush-baby and the imitation elephant.

The only natural enemy of small animals was the python. Snow White would have been happy to dine on such delicious titbits as the bush-baby, elephant shrew, colobus monkey and the two small gorillas – but, alas, she already bulged with the food that had been forced down her throat and would not be interested in anything more until that was digested.

So this strange assortment of prize animals managed to get along with each other amazingly well.

'Humans wouldn't do as well,' Hal said. 'Imagine nine different people, a Hottentot, a Masai, a hooligan, a hippie, a cannibal, a convict, a college professor, a parson and a pirate, all cooped together in this room – they'd be at each other's throats in no time. But look at what we have – a roomful of perfectly behaved ladies and gentlemen.'

'The worst is the two-legged one in the cage outside,' Roger said. Hal knew that he meant Nero.

'Well at least he won't set fire to anything tonight.'

'You think he did it last night?'

'Who else?'

Feeling quite safe, they slept – only to be roused a few hours later by a pounding on the door and shouts of 'Fire! Fire!'

They ran out to find the men already dousing the flames. The fire had started exactly where it had begun the night before – at the end of the cabin occupied by the two boys.

They joined the bucket brigade. This time there were no elephants to help them. It took an hour of hard work to extinguish the fire.

With blackened faces and pyjamas sprinkled with ashes, the boys had time now to think.

'He certainly is determined to do us in,' Hal said.

'Who?'

'Nero, of course. I suppose he's miles away by this time. I wonder how he got out of that cage. It was double-padlocked.'

'Let's go and look at the locks.'

Picking their way with the help of a flashlight, they passed through the fleet of fourteen cars to Nero's prison-on-wheels at the far edge of the camp.

The locks were still locked.

Hal was puzzled. 'That's funny. There's no other way

he could have escaped. And yet, somehow, he got out, started a fire, and made a getaway.'

'Let me have that flash,' Roger said. He played the light inside the cage. In one corner was a huddled form. It looked like a bundle of clothes.

They went around to get a closer look. The bundle of clothes was snoring. It was Nero, sound asleep.

The two amateur detectives could hardly believe their eyes. This couldn't happen – yet it had happened. Hal picked up a stick, put it between the bars and poked the sleeper. Nero woke with a start and stared into the light.

'Well, what is it?' he snapped. 'It's not enough to cage me like an animal. You have to come prodding me awake in the middle of the night.'

'You didn't make that fire?'

'What fire? If I could get out I'd give you more than fire to worry about.'

Walking back to their room, Hal muttered, 'It's too deep for me. By the way, Tieg wasn't out there helping put out that fire. I wonder . . . Oh well, there's one good thing about it. We've still got our gorilla killer and he's headed for jail in the morning.'

Morning came too soon. At the first glimmer of dawn

the bush-baby showed why it had been called a bush-baby. It started a loud, squalling cry sounding like that of a very bad-tempered baby: *Pay-yah! Pay-yah! Pay-yah! Wah-wah!* When it wasn't singing this song it filled in with crackles and grunts.

The Little Bishop, so solemn and quiet during the day, forgot all his dignity and broke into a shrill whistle that almost drowned out the bush-baby. *Whee! Whee! Whee! Listen to me.* He took gigantic leaps around the room. He soared so easily that it seemed he must have wings. His gorgeous white robe floated out behind him like a cloud. He sprang from chairback to chairback, from mantel to window, from Roger's chest to Hal's, landing on them as lightly as a bird.

The elephant shrew shrieked in a fairly good imitation of the scream of an elephant.

The chimp chattered, the baby gorillas crooned and the big female gorilla, Lady Luck, slapped herself with hollowed hands, producing a sound like the popping of corks from bottles.

The only silent member of the menagerie was Snow White. She continued the quiet process of digestion while the air rocked around her.

The boys gave up the attempt to sleep an hour

longer to make up for the hour they had lost during the night. Everybody had a good appetite for breakfast – everybody except the already stuffed python. As to what made a good breakfast, they did not agree.

The bush-baby searched the windows and roof for insects. The elephant shrew had a taste for grasshoppers. His reverence, the Bishop, preferred flowers. It seemed very appropriate that this gorgeous animal should prefer food that was both fragrant and beautiful.

The gorilla babies had to have their milk. The senior gorilla and the chimp enjoyed fruit. Rocking Horse would take nothing but dry thorns, while Flatfoot must have juicy water plants. The only one who would devour anything and everything that was brought to him was Nero. It was probably the last good meal he would have for many a day, since Congo prisons are not famous for their cuisine.

At the office of the commandant, Deputy Hal Hunt delivered his prisoner to the authorities.

He and Roger took the road back to camp in high spirits. Their enemy was behind bars. Now they would have no more trouble.

But trouble waited for them around a bend of the road.

18
Black Leopard

As they skirted the base of the active volcano they rounded a corner to find the way blocked by a green pole standing upright in the middle of the road. Hal stepped on the brakes. The car shuddered to a halt within three feet of the post.

'Now, whoever put that there?' Hal said irritably. 'No room to get around it. Hop out and pull it up.'

Luckily Roger was a bit slow. He was just about to slide out when he saw the post move. The windscreen was dusty, as it always is in Africa, and they could not see the thing plainly. But the top of the post seemed to be expanding and a red tongue darted in and out.

'But it can't be a snake,' Roger said. 'How could a snake stand six feet tall?'

'Because most of it is on the ground,' Hal said.

In the dust of the road lay nine feet of snake, easily supporting the erect six feet.

'What is it?'

'A mamba. The Africans call it The Snake that Walks on Its Tail. Wish we could get it. Isn't it a beauty?'

The mamba was grass-green and its scales sparkled like jewels. But Roger was a little too uneasy to appreciate its beauty.

He had heard too many grim stories about the mamba. It was famous for its bad temper. If you approach it slowly, it would glide away. But if you startled it, as this one had been startled by the sudden arrival of the car, it would attack.

It could strike hard enough to knock a man down. It had been known to chase and kill a man on horseback. It had a bad record for attacking people in cars. If cut in half, the front half could still attack.

'It's mighty poisonous, isn't it?'

'Nothing more deadly in Africa. You can actually drink its poison without harm. But if it gets into your veins it paralyses the respiratory system and you quit breathing.'

'What are you going to do about it?'

'Just wait a minute and see if it quiets down. Then I'll try to get it.'

They waited. The cobra-like hood grew smaller and the stiff body relaxed.

'We'll have to act quickly or it'll be gone. There's a bag in the rear of the truck. Do you think you could sneak around very quietly and get it?'

The errand did not appeal to Roger. But he cautiously opened the door. Unfortunately his nervous hand struck the handle and at the sound the snake became rigid. Then it was suddenly on the car itself where it struck the windscreen a terrific blow that cracked the glass and left it dripping with poison.

'Hope it didn't hurt its nose doing that,' Hal said.

Roger looked at Hal curiously. This was a funny brother of his who thought more about keeping a specimen in perfect condition than about the danger of getting bitten.

The snake seemed a little discouraged. It had expected to bury its fangs in flesh and blood and all it got was a whack on the nose.

'Now, while it's still dizzy, get that bag.'

Roger slipped out and returned at once with the sack. He closed the door carefully, but didn't bother with the window which was open only a crack – certainly not enough to admit a large snake.

But the mamba, exploring the window, found the crack and made use of it. This snake has the peculiar ability to flatten itself so that it may pass through a space no thicker than a sandwich.

The swiftly moving snake was well started through

the crack before the boys realized what it was up to.

'Too late to do anything about it,' Hal said. 'Keep perfectly quiet. Don't move an inch. Perhaps that bump knocked all the zing out of it and now all it wants is a dark hole to crawl into.'

'Suppose you're wrong,' said Roger. 'Do we have any serum in the car?'

'None.'

'If it bites, will there still be time to get to camp?'

'No. You'd be dead in ten minutes. Now shut up and don't move.'

The snake glided smoothly over Roger's back, giving him a prickly sensation he would never forget. He could hardly refrain from throwing it off or at least letting out a good scream, but he kept himself bottled up tightly as it passed along the back of the seat to Hal. It chose to slide over Hal's neck and then down into the sack which Hal had left invitingly open to receive it.

Hal did not breathe until all of the fifteen-foot serpent was inside the bag and well settled. Then, moving very slowly, he gave the lover of darkness a complete blackout by closing the bag and tying it shut. Now the snake was at peace. But the same could not be said for the nerves of the two animal collectors.

As they drove on towards camp their jumpy heart-beats slowed down and their spirits rose.

'Pretty good morning's work,' Hal said. 'One of Africa's most famous snakes in the bag – and Nero put away where he can do no more harm. Perhaps the gorillas can live in peace now, and so can we.'

This pleasant pipe-dream was rudely shattered when they arrived at camp and Joro came running with some bad news.

'There's been another killing,' he said. 'Twenty more gorillas dead. Nero has been at it again.'

'That's impossible,' Hal said. 'You know yourself that Nero was double-locked in a cage all last night, and now he's in jail.'

Joro shook his head. 'Then it is witchcraft.'

'Joro, you know better than that. You're too intelligent to believe in witchcraft.'

'I don't know,' Joro said. 'Perhaps there is no witchcraft in your country, but this is Africa.'

'Africa or anywhere else, there's a natural reason for everything. And I'm going to find out what it was this time. Where did this happen?'

'About one hour's walk down the elephant trail that leads to the valley.'

'After lunch I'll go and take a look.'

'I'll go with you,' Roger said.

'No, you'd better stay here and look after the animals. See that the mamba is put in a good cage. Don't let him get his fangs into you.'

After a hasty lunch, Hal set off down the trail by which the valley elephants often came at dusk to drink at the lake.

Occasionally he passed an elephant pit. These pits had been dug by Africans and were now neglected, but when new they had been covered with leafy branches through which the unsuspecting elephant would fall and remain trapped until men came to kill him and carve him up to feed the villages.

The pits were now old and uncovered and the beasts had picked their way around them. Hal did the same.

After walking for about an hour he began to look for the twenty dead gorillas. He found them at last in a small cleared space under a giant hagenia.

Hal could not understand what he saw. He was almost inclined to agree with the believers in witchcraft. There was no sign that human beings had been here – no human footprints, no broken spears or arrowheads.

Many of the bodies were torn and looked as if they

had been partly eaten. He knew that Africans sometimes do kill gorillas for their meat. But they would not have left so much behind them. They would have taken the carcasses to their villages to devour later.

There were many dead babies. That was strange. Gangsters usually killed the adults and took away the babies alive to sell to animal collectors. Here both old and young had been slaughtered.

All the adults were females. The males, if any, must have been absent on a food-hunting quest. That had made things easier for the mysterious killer, as female gorillas seldom fight. When attacked, they sit doubled over with hands protecting their heads.

Blood dripping through the leaves of the hagenia made him look up. In the branches more than a hundred feet from the ground dangled the bodies of two large gorillas. How did they get up there? Young gorillas climb trees, but adults, because of their weight, prefer to stay on the ground.

Could the two large apes have been taken aloft after they were dead? African hunters would have no reason for doing that. Not if they were human hunters. The only animal hunter that could do it and would do it was the leopard. This cat would climb a tree with a carcass twice its own weight and hang it high to ripen and tenderize before he eats it. Thus he keeps it safe from the hyenas and jackals which never climb trees.

Hal had an uneasy feeling that someone was watching him. He pivoted on his heels, scanning every bush in the circle.

There it was, just partly visible, a black face and two deep-set eyes. As he looked, it vanished.

It looked like the face of a gorilla – his sworn enemy, Gog?

Had Gog done all this? He could not believe it. Men killed men, but gorillas do not kill gorillas.

Still puzzled and distressed, he started back towards camp. Black clouds covered the sky and a heavy pall of smoke from the volcano did not improve the visibility. It was only mid-afternoon but it seemed almost night under the heavy canopy of trees. An occasional flash of lightning lit the path, but blinded the eyes so that the shadows seemed darker than before.

He kept in mind that there were elephant pits along this trail. Fortunately they had lost their cover of brush, so it should be easy, even in this dim light, to see them and go around them. So he confidently trotted along the path and was astonished when what appeared to be a bed of leaves gave way under his feet and he dropped into an elephant-sized hole.

He landed with a rude jolt but decided that he was not really hurt. He was greatly puzzled. If this pit had been concealed when he came from camp he would have fallen into it. It must have been open then and he had seen it and avoided it. It had since been covered. By whom? Had someone planned to trap him?

Whoever it was, he would fool him. With a good strong set of arms and legs, he should be able to climb out of this spot without difficulty.

But when he tried it he found that the walls were steep and offered no handhold. Besides, the pit was about twenty feet deep — as deep as a two-storey building is high. To try to clamber out would be like trying to climb the outside wall of a building without the help of a fire-escape or even a drainpipe.

But there was another way. Dangling from above was a stout vine or liana of the sort used by the Africans as rope.

He laid hold of it and began to climb hand over hand.

He had not made five feet when the vine came loose from the brush above and both vine and boy tumbled to the bottom of the pit.

Still he did not worry. It might be a long wait, but sooner or later someone would come looking for him. Joro knew what path he had taken. He would just sit down and take it easy – and hope that no elephant would be fooled as he had been and drop in on him. He moved over into a corner so that he would be less likely to get mashed if this should happen.

He dozed, in spite of flashes of lightning followed at once by thunder. But what really roused him was a sound like that of a saw going through a hardwood knot. He recognized at once the scream of a leopard.

It came again, but this time at the very edge of the pit.

He strained his eyes to see what was going on. Two dark figures seemed to be engaged in a wrestling match. One of them, he could tell by the screams, was a leopard. The other was completely silent and appeared to be trying to push the leopard over the edge.

It took a good bit of trying. The leopard seemed to be about half the size of its opponent. But the leopard is rated as the strongest animal of its size in Africa. What other animal can climb a tree with a carcass twice its own weight in its teeth?

But this time the leopard had met its match. With an ear-splitting shriek it fell into the pit.

The figure above turned away. 'Hey, you up there – help me get out of here,' Hal shouted.

He got no answer. The mysterious stranger was going. Perhaps he didn't understand English. Hal tried to say it in Swahili. Didn't the fellow have ears? Yet he calmly walked away and left Hal to deal with a very unpleasant companion.

19
Man Against Cat

Daniel in the lions' den was much safer than Hal in the company of an angry leopard.

As every visitor to animal Africa knows, you may come within fifteen feet of a lion or a whole pride of lions and suffer no harm – as long as you carry no gun and behave yourself. But you take your life in your hands if you come that close to a leopard.

The lion is a social animal. The leopard is a loner. During an African safari you will see hundreds of lions at close range. You may come away from Africa without having seen a single leopard. It is there and it has seen you, but it doesn't care for your company.

Particularly dangerous is a leopard trapped in a small space with a human. And this one was already infuriated by its fight with the dark Someone or Something.

Being a night animal, its senses of sight and smell were superhuman. It saw, smelt and hated, and for it to hate was to act. Like a flash of lightning, it charged. Hal found himself trying to stave off a raging, biting, clawing devil. No wonder this creature was called the hellcat.

By instinct it went straight for the eyes. If these could be scratched out, the rest would be easy.

Hal dodged, and the beast crashed into the corner. This did not improve its temper. It turned with a sawing scream and sank its claws into and through Hal's bush jacket. Hal tried to twist out of the way, but this snake on four legs could out-twist any man. It seemed to coil around him like a python while its jaws groped for his throat. Its own throat was now in Hal's powerful grip and was being squeezed so tightly that it could hardly breathe.

By a violent contortion it pulled itself free. But Hal was moving at the same instant and managed to turn the cat on its back. He got his knees on its lungs. His elbows planted in its armpits spread its front legs apart so that he could not be torn by its claws.

But he was not paying proper attention to his hands. By a swift lunge the leopard caught his right between its jaws. Hal's efforts to pull it away were in vain.

Then Hal remembered. Carl Akeley, the man who lay buried near the cabin, had once been in the same predicament. Unable to pull his hand free, he had turned the tables upon his opponent by doing what the leopard least expected. The leopard was used to hanging onto a

limb that tried to free itself. But suppose the arm or leg between its jaws went in the opposite direction.

Every time the teeth relaxed their hold for a moment, Akeley, instead of trying to jerk his hand free, forced it farther into the animal's throat. So he actually choked it to death.

Hal followed the example of the master. Each time the teeth eased up on his hand he drove his fist deeper. At the same time his left hand bore down heavily on the animal's throat. His knees forced the air out of the beast's lungs.

But how long could he keep this up? Black patches were flickering across his eyes and he felt sick. He was weakening fast.

It seemed for ever. Did this cat, like others, have nine lives? How long could it fight without air? The right fist and the left hand completely cut off its wind, yet it struggled.

A flash from the sky gave light for an instant, and Hal could not believe what he saw. Or rather what he did not see. He seemed to be fighting nothing but a black shadow. He could almost believe that the whole thing was only a product of his crazed imagination.

The flash should have revealed a writhing creature in black and yellow. No animal's coat is more conspicuous – yet Hal had seen nothing.

Then it was that it occurred to him that he must take this animal alive. For here was no ordinary leopard. This was the very rare all-black leopard sometimes called a panther that every zoo wanted but few ever got.

Akeley had kept up the suffocation technique until the beast died. To take it alive would be more difficult. Hal dared not leave off too soon, and he must not keep it up too long. Just how much was enough?

Not being accustomed to choking animals, he had no experience to go by.

The animal stopped struggling and became limp. Its jaws relaxed. The lungs under Hal's knees stopped pumping. Would the animal promptly revive if allowed to breathe?

Hal withdrew a bleeding arm and fist and relieved the weight on the leopard's chest. He waited a moment, ready to repeat the choking process, but there was no movement. For all he knew, his prize might be dead.

Where was that liana? He fished about for it, found it, tied the rear feet, tied the front feet, then tied all four together.

He waited anxiously for signs of life. He felt for the heart – it was still beating, but slowly, as if it could not make up its mind whether to recover or quit.

His hand over the animal's nose detected a slight movement of air. Now Hal was sure. He could have sung and danced – if he had not been so frightfully tired.

The leopard sawed faintly. It began a snake-like squirming. Soon it was thrashing about violently and Hal thought best to retreat to the other side of the pit. There he collapsed and, thinking he must remained awake until help came, he promptly went to sleep.

He was roused by his brother's voice and the glare of flashlights.

'What are you doing down there?' Roger demanded.

'Just putting in time,' Hal said. 'Got a rope?'

A rope end was lowered to him. He noosed it around the leopard's feet. 'Haul away.'

The men hauled, and were surprised to find at the end of the line not the man they had expected but a sprawling, spitting, growling black leopard.

Again they let down the rope. Hal ordinarily would have swarmed up it like a sailor. Now he had hardly enough energy to make a loop for his foot and hang on while he was hoisted like a bale of hay. He dropped in a heap on the grass.

'I'll be ready to walk in a few minutes.'

'Walk nothing,' Roger said. 'Anybody who can take on a panther single-handed deserves to ride.'

So Hal and the leopard got equal honours. The leopard was borne on a pole thrust between its legs, and Hal on a hastily-made bamboo litter.

Arriving at the cabin, Hal was immediately laid out

on his bed where Roger and Joro carefully washed out his wounds, pumped them full of antiseptic, and applied bandages.

Then Roger went out to see to the unbinding and caging of the leopard. The men marvelled over the trophy. Most of them had never before seen a black leopard.

'It must be pretty rare,' Roger said upon returning to Hal's bedside. 'What's it worth?'

'Five times as much as the yellow-and-black.'

'Aren't you exaggerating?'

'Not a bit. Almost everybody has seen the spotted leopard, or pictures of it. But here's a novelty – like our white python. Or a white tiger.'

'Is there such a thing as a white tiger?'

'Crandon Park Zoo in Miami has a yellow-and-black tiger and a white tiger. The first is valued at twelve hundred dollars and the white carries a price of thirty-five thousand dollars – just because everybody is familiar with the regular but not one person in perhaps a million has ever laid eyes on a white.'

'One thing I don't understand,' Roger said. 'Of course I can see why a bonehead like you fell into a hole

'Thank you,' Hal said.

'But I wouldn't think anything as smart as a leopard would fall in.'

'It didn't fall in. It was pushed.'

'Who could have done that?'

'How should I know? It was too dark to see him plainly. It couldn't have been Nero – he's in jail. The fellow was about the size of Tieg – but Tieg was here in camp. At least I suppose he was. It could have been one of the trouble-makers who are out to kill all the whites. Or it could have been Gog.'

'Why should Gog do that?'

'Because he thinks we killed his family. And because a festering bullet-wound has made a rogue out of him.'

'But pushing a leopard in to kill you – that took planning. And we used to be told in school that animals don't plan. They just act by instinct.'

Hal laughed weakly. 'That idea is old-hat. Sure, animals do lots of things by instinct, just as we humans do. We chew by instinct, swallow by instinct, do a thousand things by instinct. But we can plan too, and so can the higher animals. Jane Goodall, who lived with the chimps not far from here, gave them problems that were quite new to them and they solved them.'

'But chimps are smarter than gorillas.'

'That's another notion that is not borne out by facts. Chimps seem smarter, because they are great performers. They like to show off and they love applause. There's as much difference between a chimp and a gorilla as there is between a comedian and a judge. The chimp does all sorts of tricks for the fun of it. The gorilla sits and thinks. He can do things that need to be done but he doesn't do them just to amuse you. Schaller, the fellow who lived in this cabin while he was studying gorillas, found that they were very bright, in their quiet way. When they wanted to they could use tools, wash clothes, dig sweet potatoes, open doors, turn a screw to the right to tighten it and to the left to loosen it, eat with a spoon, build bridges over streams, pound nuts with a hammer, dip sugar in water to soften it, use a lever, make rope, drive in a nail, use a knife and fork, ride a bicycle and even drive a car. But they are shy – they won't do any of these things just to show off. They have a good memory for what they have done, and plan what to do tomorrow.'

'So you really think Gog could have covered that pit so you would fall in, and tossed in the leopard to kill you.'

'I didn't say that. I just said that if he wanted to, he

189

could. And I wouldn't blame him a bit – considering what he thinks we've done to him.'

There was a banging on the door. 'Come in,' Roger said. Joro thrust in his head.

'You wanted a spitting cobra. We've just found one.'

Hal tried to get up, but fell back. 'Lie still,' Roger commanded. 'We'll get it.'

As he went out the door Hal called after him, 'Watch your eyes.'

It was a strange thing to say, Roger thought. He supposed Hal meant, 'Keep your eyes open.' Perhaps his brother was a little light-headed, as anyone might be after a tussle with a big cat.

20
Spitting Cobra

Roger didn't know too much about cobras. Of course he had seen them in his father's collection and in zoos, but they had been the sort used by Indian snake-charmers.

The African spitting cobra was new to him. The name itself told him it could spit, but how far, and how well, he did not know.

Who cares if it spits? he thought as he ran with Joro. It's the snakes that bite that you have to be afraid of.

Passing the supply truck, he snatched up a forked stick, lasso and bag. He had seen his brother use these things and it had not looked difficult. It didn't occur to him to be afraid. What he lacked in knowledge he made up in nerve.

At the west end of the clearing the men stood in a circle around the snake. It was a wide circle – no man ventured closer than twenty feet to the serpent. It stood five feet tall, its beady eyes and darting tongue warning these meddlesome humans to keep their distance.

It was a beauty, if you could think of snakes as beautiful. Its jet-black hood was spread a good eight inches wide. Below the black was a sun-white neck. The rest of the body was a mosaic of round discs in perfect rows as if designed by a fine artist.

The men, who had expected Hal, were surprised by Roger's arrival, but quite willing to leave the capture of the snake to him. They would tackle a non-poisonous python, but had good reason to dread the deadly venom of a cobra. They knew how to kill snakes, but not how to take them alive, and had no wish to learn. If these crazy white men wanted live snakes, it was up to them to take them.

Here again was a snake that 'walked on its tail'. Not, of course, on the end of its tail, but on the rear part of its body while the fore part stood erect. Actually, such a snake walks on its ribs. Each rib is movable – it slides ahead, takes hold, pulls the body forward, then repeats.

The cobra was doing just that – rib-walking back and forth, always holding its head high, watching for a way of escape.

It was so occupied in watching the enemies around that it failed to notice the one above. But Roger saw it and was fascinated.

'What a weirdo!'

The hornbill was indeed weird, a great, bulky creature

nearly four feet long in black, white, red and yellow. It had a terrible nutcracker of a bill a foot long and on top of the bill was a great hollow helmet that serves as an echo chamber so that every time the creature croaks, laughs, trumpets, or caws, the sound is magnified four or five times as if by a loudspeaker.

Roger knew the bird by reputation – how the female lays one large egg in a hollow tree and her husband shuts her in by plugging the entrance with clay leaving only one small hole through which he can feed her while she incubates the egg and cares for the baby.

She willingly stays in this prison for five months, never once stirring outside, while her mate stuffs insects, fruit and – best of all – chunks of snake meat through the hole.

For the hornbill is death to snakes and will attack even the most poisonous.

This one, seated on a branch above the cobra, was peering down at it with great interest. Doubtless he was saying to himself, 'Mama would like that!'

Suddenly he dropped with a loud laugh like that of a hyena and his nutcracker closed on the snake's neck just behind its head. At once the snake came to life, wrestling to reach the bird with its fangs. The enormous

wings began to flap and in another instant would have carried both bird and serpent away to the waiting wife.

Both of them were well off the ground when the loop of Roger's lasso settled down upon them, binding together the snake's neck and the bill of the bird.

This was a little more than Roger wanted. Plenty of zoos had hornbills. Besides, he had a mental picture of mother and infant waiting patiently for the return of their provider.

When the bird struggled to free itself of the noose, he did not draw it too tightly. The hornbill drew out its nutcracker and flapped away. He was not laughing now. With his best booming voice he was telling the whole world what he thought of boys with lassoes.

Now what? Roger had the snake noosed, but if he pulled the snake towards him it might make a sudden lunge and bite.

It would be hard to use the forked stick. That is good if the snake's head is flat on the ground. Then you may pin it down by the fork, one prong on each side, and hold it still while you grasp the neck. But how do you fork a head swaying in mid air?

Roger tried time and again. He could get the head in

the fork, but when he tried to bring it to the ground it would slip out.

And the snake was becoming more and more angry. Its eyes were fixed on its tormentor and the hood was expanded to its full width. That meant it was fighting mad.

Roger thought he was playing it safe. He kept at least ten feet between him and the cobra. Certainly he couldn't be bitten at that distance.

'It's going to spit,' Joro warned.

'Let it spit. It can't shoot this far.'

'Look out! Close your eyes.'

What was Joro afraid of? Many animals, such as the cats, could spit. Perhaps a foot or two. Anyhow, the spit was harmless.

In the next instant the young naturalist learned a lesson he would never forget. Two white streams shot out from the snake's poison fangs like bullets fired from a double-barrelled gun. Instead of losing their speed after going a foot or two, they covered the ten feet between snake and boy in a fraction of a second and exactly hit their target – Roger's two eyes.

He would never have believed it possible. How could the snake project so far and with such accuracy? It might have splashed his bush jacket, or missed him entirely. How did it know that the tenderest part of an enemy was the eye?

He brushed the moisture away with the back of his hand. It did no good. Enough had penetrated to give him intense pain. It was as if hot irons were digging out his eyes. Worst of all, he found himself half blind. The trees, the men, the snake, all blended in one great agonizing blur.

He was not aware that he had slacked up on the line. The cobra at once tried to make good its escape but Toto was in its way. The frantic snake bit him on the arm. The fangs went deep and the venom was still plentiful and potent.

Roger dimly realized what had happened. Though aching, twitching, burning up, he jumped to save Toto from a very quick death. He gave the line to Joro, first slashing off a yard of rope. He stumbled over to Toto and tied the rope around his arm just above the bite as a tourniquet. He staggered towards the supply truck and fell. Two men helped him to his feet and stayed with him. He blundered about, finally got his hands on the Fitzsimmons snake kit and was helped back to Toto who lay on the ground jerking convulsively.

Roger, though unacquainted with the spitting cobra, did know something about snakebite and how to treat it. He drew out his knife. Toto's arm swam before his eyes. He couldn't see the fang wounds. A man had to guide his hand.

He cut a deep criss-cross through each puncture and rubbed in permanganate crystals. Then his hand searched the kit for the hypodermic. With a wobbling uncertainty that would have disgraced any doctor he finally got the needle into the flesh of the bite area and injected the antivenom serum.

'Take him to the cabin,' he said. 'Lay him out and keep him quiet.'

Now his greatest desire was to faint. And lose the cobra? He tried to look through the clouds that seemed to cover his eyes.

'Where is it – the snake?'

Joro pulled it over within reach. Roger knew he must hurry to get this thing done before he blacked out completely. He didn't bother about the forked stick. He wasn't afraid of the snake now – it must have used up its venom in its double attack. He groped for its neck. Again a black hand guided his. He clutched the neck just behind the head.

'The bag,' he demanded.

It was put in his hands. Now he got plenty of help. While he firmly held the neck, the men stuffed the tail and body into the bag. Then Roger thrust in the head and closed the bag.

Roger, with his job done, now thought he had a right to faint. When he came to he was lying on his bed and something was pouring into his eyes. At first he thought the snake was giving him another shot. He put up his hands to cover his eyes.

'Lie still,' Hal commanded, and the pouring continued.

'What's that?'

'Condensed milk.'

'Are you crazy? What good is that?'

'It won't do much good,' Hal admitted. 'But it will help to relieve the pain and neutralize the poison.'

'Poison? It was just spit.'

'It was pure poison,' Hal said. 'The poison glands are just back of the fangs. Strong muscles shoot it out through the fangs. It works like a water pistol. Except that it's a lot more accurate than a water pistol. The spitting cobra is the only creature on earth, so far as I know, that carries a gun in its mouth. Steady. I'm going to give you an injection.'

'But you already dosed me with milk.'

'That was just for the eyes. This is for the rest of you. The poison must have travelled through your whole system.' Roger felt the sharp prick of the hypodermic needle.

'How's Toto?' Roger asked.

'He'll come round. It's you I'm worried about. You got the full dose – Toto only got what was left. You're a lucky boy.'

'Lucky?'

'Lucky not to be totally and permanently blind. How do things look to you?'

Roger screwed his eyes open. 'Where are you?'

'Right over you. Within two feet of your face.'

'You look like a bad dream.'

'Good. That's better than looking like nothing at all. I don't suppose there's a single village in cobra country without at least one person stumbling around blind as a bat for the rest of his life, thanks to the spitting cobra.'

'How do the Africans treat it?'

'By magic. I can't say much for milk but at least it's better than magic'

All night Roger squirmed, twitched and twisted. Every nerve in his body screamed. He wanted to let the scream get out, but firmly kept his mouth shut. Spasms and cramps doubled him up. His heart throbbed and his head seemed about to explode. He couldn't sleep. It seemed the longest night of his life.

Hal gave him the milk treatment every hour. Hal himself was not too comfortable. He was dead tired after his tussle with the black leopard and his wounds burned.

He was surprised to hear Roger do a good imitation of a laugh. 'A fine pair of hunters we are,' Roger said. 'Both of us pretty well banged up. I'm tired of it. I've decided I'm going to be all right in the morning.'

'Hold that thought,' Hal said.

Perhaps it was the thought as much as the milk that helped to restore Roger. Anyhow, he felt much better when day came. He could see the sunlit window. He could even see Hal and the other occupants of the cabin. The two young gorillas were snuggled up against him, one on each side. Their warmth, and their affection for him, were comforting.

The dance of jangled nerves had died down. His head, which had been off all night, had somehow got screwed on again. He had wanted nothing more than to go home to good safe Long Island and be babied by his mother and father. Now the man in him was coming to life again. He even began to plan the day.

'Hal, are you awake?'

Foolish question. 'Sure,' said Hal, who had not closed his eyes all night.

'The men were telling me about a snake with two heads. They know where its nest is. Shouldn't we go get it?'

21
Snake with Two Heads

Poor kid, thought Hal. He must be having a nightmare. Two heads, indeed!

He raised himself on his elbow to get a better look. Roger's eyes were wide open.

'You're talking nonsense, little brother,' he said. 'Get some more sleep. Snakes don't come with two heads.'

'But the men said . . .'

'They made a mistake. Perhaps they saw two heads. But they must have belonged to two different snakes. How do you feel this morning?'

'A lot better. Thanks for milking me all night. Things are kind of hazy yet, but my eyes don't ache the way they did. About the snake – ask Joro.'

To humour the boy, Hal went to the door and called Joro.

'My brother is still a bit out of his mind. He's talking about a snake with two heads. Says you saw one.'

'Yes, bwana. We saw one. Its nest is in a tree.'

More and more absurd, thought Hal. A two-headed

snake with a nest in a tree instead of a hole in the ground. Whoever heard of such a thing?

Something began to stir in his memory. He pulled out his reptile manual and looked up not 'snakes', nor 'nests', but 'Siamese twins'.

Yes, here it was. Not only humans could be Siamese twins, but animals too. Sometimes it was a matter of two bodies and one head. Sometimes, two heads and one body.

Scientists had learned much about the operation of the brain by studying the behaviour of two-headed snakes such as the king snake found on the beach at Del Mar, California, in 1967, which was made at home in the Reptile House of the San Diego Zoo. It was the second two-headed snake to be shown in this zoo and there were two or three to be found in other zoos, but so rarely that such a specimen was of great scientific and popular interest and brought a very high price.

Animal collector Hal Hunt's enthusiasm was at once aroused. 'I want to see this thing.'

'Me too,' came from Roger's bed.

The two invalids creaked and groaned a good deal as they dressed, but forgot their aches when Joro took them to the acacia tree where the double-headed snake made its home.

Before them was one of the most astonishing sights in Africa. The wide-spreading, flat-topped tree was like an enormous chandelier with dozens of globes hanging from every branch. They were not glass globes and contained no light, but were made of dry grass, golden-yellow, seeming to glow in the light of the early sun.

'Weavers' nests,' exclaimed Hal.

Roger looked at them in amazement. So this was the work of the famous weaver birds. They deserved their name. They had done a beautiful job of weaving the yellow grasses to make nests that could not be blown away by any windstorm.

'There must be two or three hundred in that one tree.'

'More than that,' Hal said. 'Closer to five hundred. But that isn't many. In Rhodesia twelve hundred nests were counted in one tree.'

'And a family in each nest?'

'No. One family in two nests. The male does all the building. First he weaves a nest for his mate where she can lay her eggs and care for the chicks. Then he makes another nest for himself.'

'So much work!'

'Yes, but he seems to love doing it. Just as anybody is happy doing something he can do well.'

'But why so many nests in one tree when the forest is full of trees?'

'The weaver is a very sociable bird. It likes company and plenty of it. Besides, if there are a lot of birds together they can beat off their enemies more easily.'

'Speaking of enemies, where's that snake?'

Joro pointed out a nest close to the tree-trunk. It lives there. Killed the bird and stole its nest.'

Joro prodded the nest with the noosing pole he had brought from camp. With a hissing sound a head popped out, then another. They seemed to be competing with each other to see which could hiss more loudly. The heads were followed by five feet of handsome and colourful body. Even with one head, the snake would have attracted attention in any zoo.

'A boomslang!' Hal exclaimed.

'A what slang?'

'Boomslang. Funny name, but it just means tree snake.'

'Is it poisonous?'

'The Africans say yes. The naturalists who have tested it in the laboratories say no.'

'Perhaps one head is poisonous and the other isn't,' joked Roger. 'Is that possible?'

'Anything is possible in this strange world. Of course there's a way you can find out. Let both heads bite you and see what happens.'

'Thank you,' Roger said. 'After what happened yesterday, I'm steering clear of snake poison for a while.'

'Give it another poke, Joro,' Hal said. 'Perhaps it will put on its special act.'

The result was a surprise even to Hal. The poke had a different effect upon the two heads. One head didn't notice it because its eyes were fixed upon a bird. The other head was watching the men. Seeing the stick coming and feeling it, the annoyed brain telegraphed its neck muscles and the neck swelled until it looked like a toy balloon.

'Just like the puffer fish,' Roger said. In his underwater work he had seen this harmless-looking fish blow itself up to ten times its usual size when it wanted to frighten away its enemies. But here were two brains quite independent of each other. One was angry and the other was only interested in dinner.

The hungry head darted at the bird, caught it, and swallowed it. One could see the bulge going down the neck and into the stomach. There the food would be digested and would feed both brains.

Roger wished he had two heads. Then one could work and the other play. Or one could keep watch when they were on safari, and the other sleep. One could mind Dad and the other could do as it pleased. A pretty neat arrangement.

But it might be inconvenient at times. Suppose one wanted to go fishing and the other wanted to stay at home and read. Suppose one liked water skiing and the other preferred to climb a mountain. With such different ideas, there was a good chance that he would tear himself apart.

'You'd think the two heads would agree since they are Siamese twins,' he said.

'It doesn't work that way,' Hal said. 'Human twins don't think alike. One may be jolly and light-hearted, and the other may be as sour as a pickle. One may be very clever and the other stupid. It's the same way in snakedom. In San Diego one head of the king snake became very tame while the other head would try to attack the keeper every time he came near.'

The boomslang wormed one head deep into a nest and came out with a bird in its teeth. Its brother head seized the other end of the bird and the two began a tug-of-war. It looked as if their victim would be torn apart in the middle. But finally the bird managed to free itself and flew away, squawking loudly.

Each head seemed to blame the other for what had happened. The air from the lungs inflated the two windpipes until they became the size of footballs. The two heads faced each other, mouths open, tongues darting in and out. Each head tried to bite the other, but the angry footballs were in the way.

'Snakes don't have a very highly developed brain,' Hal

said. 'It doesn't occur to these quarrelsome heads that they can't bite each other unless they first let the air out of their balloons. So as long as their anger lasts they are protected against each other. But watch – one of them is giving up. It's trying to get away. Its balloon is going down because it's no longer angry, but just frightened.'

The tough-minded head had now got its teeth into the timid head.

Hal couldn't stand by and see his beautiful specimen mangle itself. 'It's time we put a stop to this. Joro, give me the pole.'

At the far end of the pole was a loop and the rope ran down the pole to Hal's hand. If he could get the loop over the snake's heads he could draw the rope tight and bring down the snake.

The first attempt was not too successful. The noose caught one head only. Hal tried to pull the snake from the branch but the free head bit into the bark and held on.

'Pull harder,' said Roger. 'Let me try.'

'No, we must not pull any harder. See that webbing just where the two necks join? That's the tenderest part of the snake. Every time the two heads try to move in different directions, there's a strain on that webbing. That's the reason most two-headed snakes don't live long. When the two brains get different ideas about where they want to go, there's a severe strain at that point. I've got to get the noose over both heads.'

Now both of the serpent's brains had one idea – to escape. Hal removed the loop and the snake slithered away along the branch. Hal pursued it, placed the loop before it, and both heads went through it before they realized what was happening. The noose was drawn tight.

Now that there was no danger of pulling the body apart, both boys laid hold of the pole and a good strong tug brought down the snake.

They returned to camp, the pole over Hal's shoulder with the snake dangling from the tight loop and tying itself into knots, its two neck-pouches stretched to their greatest size.

It was placed in a cage on a catching car. It was thrashing about in a fury of excitement. Each head tried a different way of escape and there was serious danger that the prize would be ripped down the middle.

'I'll put a stop to that,' Hal said.

From a roll of adhesive tape he tore off a length of two or three feet. He opened the cage just far enough to admit his hand. A lunge of a head, and the hand was bitten. Now Hal would learn for himself whether or not a boomslang was poisonous.

He didn't stop to find out. He gripped the snake just below its balloons and quickly bound the tape around the body where the two necks joined. Then he withdrew his hand and closed the cage.

'Now it can't tear itself in two.'

'But why did you use elastic tape?'

'So it can still swallow birds, rats, mice or whatever we feed it. But the elastic won't stretch enough to allow any strain on the webbing.'

Roger looked at Hal's bleeding hand. 'It's nothing,' Hal said.

But just to make sure, Roger insisted upon washing the hand, applying antiseptic, and a bandage.

'Listen,' Hal said. 'What's all that screaming?'

'Seems to be coming from our room,' Roger said.

They ran to the cabin. They flung open the door just in time to see Andre Tieg give Sam the chimp a vicious kick in the stomach. The whole menagerie was going wild. The chimp, the colobus, the bush-baby, the elephant shrew, the large gorilla and the two small ones all were screaming, roaring, whistling or beating the floor. Even

Snow White, the python, was hissing with a sound like escaping steam.

'What are you doing here?' Hal demanded.

Tieg turned to face him. He drew himself up. His yellow moustache flared and his glass eye glared.

'Mind how you speak to me,' he said. 'Someone had to look after the animals while you were fooling away your time catching snakes.'

'They don't sound as if they like the way you were taking care of them. Why did you kick that chimp?'

'That's the only way to deal with animals. Punish them when they don't behave.'

'How did he misbehave?'

'The colobus bit me. When I tried to slap him down, the chimp got in my way.'

Hal remembered how they had named the chimp the Good Samaritan, Sam for short, because he had rescued the colobus on the slopes of the volcano. Here again the good-hearted Samaritan had protected the monkey.

But the chimp was in no gentle mood now. Still screaming, he suddenly attacked Tieg from the rear and Hal had to pull him off. He got no thanks from Tieg.

'Let me deal with him,' Tieg demanded. 'I'll teach him what's what.'

'Be careful. He might teach you.'

'That shrimp? Don't be ridiculous. I could twist him around my little finger.'

'Do you want to try?'

'Any time.'

'How about right now?'

'You're inviting trouble,' Tieg warned him. 'Your precious chimp is going to get killed.'

'We'll take a chance on that. Come outside.'

Sam, still screaming, did his best to lay hold of his enemy but Hal kept him out of reach. 'You'll get your innings pretty soon, little fellow,' he said.

22
Tieg Tumbles

The hooting and screaming of the angry chimp could have been heard a mile away. The men had come to see what was the matter. They were waiting as Hal and the others came out of the cabin.

'Gather round, boys,' Tieg said. 'You're going to see some fun.' He was happy to have an audience.

Hal let Sam go. The chimp and the man who had kicked him faced each other.

They did not look well matched. The contrast between them made Tieg laugh. He stood well over six feet. Sam's head was on a level with his belt. The man weighed about two hundred and fifty pounds, the ape ninety-five.

'Tieg will murder him,' worried Roger.

Hal didn't worry. He knew that most of the chimp's weight was concentrated in his arms and chest. Even as Sam stood erect, his great hairy arms reached nearly to the ground.

Tieg swung his heavily booted right foot. This time the chimp didn't wait for it. He dived over it and his

hard skull came ploughing into Tieg's midriff with the force of a pile-driver. Tieg grunted, and because one foot was still in the air, he lost his balance and fell over backwards.

The chimp danced about him, screaming with rage, face distorted, eyes savage, fingernails making a sound like electric sparking as they ripped across the coarse hairs on his arms, the typical gesture of a furious chimpanzee. But he allowed Tieg to get up before he struck again.

Tieg's foot swung again but Sam was too fast for him. The chimp leaped straight up six feet in the air and landed his foot on Tieg's jaw. He was down in time to seize the man's swinging foot and tumble him again to the ground. Halfway up, Tieg felt the animal's long canine teeth sink into his leg. At the same time the powerful hands seized his proud moustache and tore half of it out by the roots.

Tieg, again on the ground, felt something hard and cold under his hand. It was an iron bar from a cage door. He leaped to his feet and brought the bar down with full force on the chimp's head – or where the head had been. The bar struck the ground. The chimp seized it with his huge hands, tore it away from Tieg, and bent it so that the muscles of his upper arms swelled to great balls. He twisted the bar into a ring and threw it away.

Then Sam began to undress Tieg. He ripped his shirt into rags and tore at his shorts with his two hands while his feet pounded the big fellow's sides. He seemed to fight as well upside-down as right side up.

He got Tieg down again and rolled him around like a log. Tieg wound up on his stomach with the ape jumping up and down on his back.

'Call off this devil,' Tieg pleaded.

Hal spoke quietly to the chimp. At the sound of his voice the animal stopped his frenzied dance, came to Hal, and took his hand. He looked up at Hal questioningly as if to say, 'Was it all right?'

'It was all right,' Hal said. 'He won't bother you again.'

Roger was surprised. 'What a quick change,' he said. 'He's as gentle as a lamb now.'

Tieg was sitting up, examining his leg where the great canines had made bloody holes. Sam let go Hal's hand and stooped beside the injured leg. He showed every sign of distress and sympathy. He was again the Good Samaritan.

Several times he had carefully observed Hal washing a wound. Now he could make use of what he had learned. He looked around for a rag. His eyes lit on Tieg's torn shirt. He ripped off a piece, ran to the lake, came back with the cloth dripping wet and gently bathed the bloody leg. Then he allowed Hal to sterilize the wound and apply a bandage.

'A very forgiving ape,' Roger said.

'It's not unusual,' said Hal. 'Chimps are like that. A full-grown chimp is subject to violent fits of temper. But they forget their tantrums just as suddenly and their usual sunny nature comes through.'

Roger picked up the iron ring. He got blue in the face trying to straighten it out. 'I never would have believed a chimp could be so strong.'

'Ever hear of Noell's boxing chimp?' Roger shook his head. 'A showman named Noell,' Hal went on, 'took an exhibition called Noell's Ark all over America playing at fairs and carnivals. The big feature of the show was a boxing match. His chimpanzee named Joe would box and wrestle all-comers and Noell offered five dollars to anyone who could get the chimp down and keep one of his shoulders on the floor for one second. Famous boxers and wrestlers tried it, but in four hundred tries not one man succeeded. Noell never had to pay out the five bucks. Which reminds me of another show featuring a six-year-old male chimp called Peter. He was as smart as he was strong. He could go through fifty-six acts in correct order without one word from his trainer. He walked out on the stage, bowed to the audience, took off his cap, sat down and ate a meal with knife and fork, brushed his teeth, combed his hair, powdered his face, gave the waiter a tip, went through a lot of other tricks, and wound up riding a bicycle furiously around the stage while drinking a glass of water and waving a flag. Then he dismounted, bowed to the audience, clapped his hands and walked out.'

Mali came to say that three monkeys had just been taken. 'Shall we keep them?'

Hal and Roger went to see them. 'Vervets,' Hal said. The wiry little creatures were chasing each other gaily around the cage.

'One thing I don't understand,' Roger said. 'The gorilla and the chimp – you call them apes. You call these monkeys. What's the difference between a monkey and an ape?'

'Difference in the way they're put together,' Hal said. 'The ape's brain is more complex.'

'You mean he's smarter?'

'Right.'

'But these monkeys look just as smart to me. They're even livelier than Sam and Lady Luck.'

'Well, suppose we test them,' Hal suggested. 'Mali, bring me some empty bottles – and a bag of peanuts.'

He selected three bottles with small necks and poured some peanuts into each. He set them inside the cage.

At once each vervet scrambled down and plunged a hand into a bottle. It clutched a handful of the nuts. But then it could not withdraw the hand. And it was not willing to drop the nuts so that the hand could be drawn out.

It was too much of a puzzle for the monkeys to solve. Chattering helplessly, they looked quite ridiculous dangling bottles from their closed hands.

'Now let's try the chimp.' Sam was presented with a bottle with a neck large enough so that he could get his hand in, but, once full of nuts, it could not be withdrawn. When he failed to remove his fist he did not chatter and dance about, waving his bottle. He sat still and did some serious thinking.

Having considered the matter, he let go of the nuts and took out his hand. Then he tipped the jar upside down, poured out the nuts, and proceeded to eat them.

'That's what a few more convolutions in the brain will do,' Hal said. 'Now the gorilla. We'll give her a slightly harder test.'

Lady Luck, looking in between the bars, studied the three monkeys still struggling to get their full fists out of the bottles. She was a sympathetic soul. She had already mothered the two baby gorillas.

She wanted to help these simple-minded vervets but must reason out a way to do it.

Finally she climbed into the supply truck and came out with a banana. She inserted it between the bars and laid it on the floor of the cage.

The monkeys stopped their chattering and prancing and looked at the fruit. To their taste, a banana was much more to be desired than nuts. Their fists relaxed, the nuts fell out, they pulled out their hands and made a dive for the banana.

'Good old Lady Luck,' Roger exclaimed. 'She really figured it out, didn't she?'

'That's it,' Hal said. 'Figuring it out – that's the main difference between monkey and ape. Don't get the idea that the monkey isn't smart. But when it comes to real thinking, the ape's brain is just a bigger and better computer.'

23
Diamonds

There was a commotion at the edge of the forest. Then Joro and some of the men came out with two prisoners.

They were white men. They carried guns. They were brought face to face with Hal and Roger.

'I think they were after gorillas,' Joro said.

The unwilling visitors were very angry. 'Take your hands off,' one of them demanded. 'Let us speak to the boss of this outfit.'

'The boss stands before you,' Joro said.

The man looked scornfully at Hal. 'What, this boy?'

If Hal was offended he did not show it. 'Let go of them,' he said.

The men released their prisoners but stood ready to seize them again if they should try to escape.

Hal looked at their guns. 'Do you have a hunting licence?'

'What business is it of yours?'

'I'm a sort of deputy sheriff for this area. Let me see your licence. You are hunting, aren't you?'

'Yes, we're hunting. But we're not hunting animals.'

'What else is there to hunt?'

'Diamonds.'

'Diamonds! Do you hunt diamonds with guns?'

The guns are just for protection. Now, young man, who the devil are you?'

'My name is Hunt – Hal Hunt. This is my brother, Roger.'

The prisoner's manner changed.

'The animal collectors,' he said. 'We know you by reputation. Allow us to introduce ourselves.'

They drew cards from their wallets and handed them over. According to the cards, these gentlemen were Robert Ryan and Tom Sims, geologists from the Williamson Diamond Mines.

'We must apologize', Hal said, 'for giving you such a rough reception. Our men thought you were poachers. Toto, tell the cook to bring some coffee.'

Seated at the outside table, the guests explained their mission.

'We've been sent out to locate new deposits of diamonds,' said Ryan.

Hal looked puzzled. 'I'm afraid I don't know much about diamond mining except that some of the mining is done four thousand feet under the surface. How do you expect to find diamonds by just roaming around the country?'

'That's the way diamonds were found in the first place,' Ryan said. 'One day some children playing on the banks of the Orange River in South Africa found a very hard pebble that was brighter than any they had ever seen. There were bright spots on the surface where the outer skin was rubbed thin, and these spots shone as though there were a hidden light, inside.

'They showed it to a neighbour. He offered to buy it. They laughed, and said he could have it for nothing.

'He took it to a store in town. The storekeeper looked at it and said, "It's a pretty pebble – but nobody would pay good money for it."

'But a man in a bigger town who really knew diamonds bought it and sold it to the governor of the colony for twenty-five hundred dollars.

'Two years later the same neighbour heard of a poor shepherd boy who had found a bright stone and carried it around as a charm. He persuaded the boy to sell it for five hundred sheep, ten head of cattle, and a horse. To the poor boy this seemed like very great wealth. But it was only a very small part of what the stone was worth. The new owner sold it for fifty-six thousand dollars.

'That started the diamond rush. People came from all over the world to hunt for diamonds. Today ninety-eight per cent of the world's diamonds come from Africa. Not just South Africa – there are rich deposits of diamonds right here in the Congo. There must be hundreds of other deposits that we don't know about. So keep your eyes open.'

'You mean we are apt to find diamonds lying on the surface?' Hal said.

'Exactly. And underneath there would be more. A deposit might run down thousands of feet. We would take those near the top by what is called open-pit mining. Farther down it would be a job of underground mining, with tunnels and shafts and lifts to bring the crystals to the surface. Our company would pay large royalties to anyone who discovered new deposits.'

'It sounds fascinating,' Hal said. 'We'll watch the ground from now on. But we can't neglect our real job. You know, we too are looking for treasure. Would you like to see some of our diamonds?'

'You have diamonds?'

'Yes. Some with four legs, some with two, some with none.'

The geologists forgot their own search as the boys took

them about to see Rocking Horse, the kudu; Flatfoot, the sitatunga; the mamba, which obligingly demonstrated its ability to stand six feet tall; the chimpanzee that had won the name of Good Samaritan; the three lively vervet monkeys.

When they went to visit the spitting cobra, Hal said, 'Don't go closer than fifteen feet.'

'Why?' asked Sims. 'It's in a cage, what could it do to us?'

'I'll show you,' Hal said. He sent Roger for a mirror. He hung it on the end of a stick and held it out within twelve feet of the cobra. The sun struck it and dazzled the eyes of the snake. Its hood expanded angrily and then a double stream of venom shot from its two fangs straight as an arrow over the twelve-foot gap and struck the very centre of the mirror.

'If your eyes had been where the mirror is,' Hal said, 'you wouldn't feel very comfortable right now. In fact if you didn't get treatment immediately you would be blinded for life.'

'Marvellous,' Ryan said. 'I didn't know the cobra could do that.'

'Most of them can't. There are ten species of cobra. This is the so-called spitting cobra. It's believed to be the only snake on earth with this talent.'

'You did well to get it,' Ryan said. 'Quite a prize – I don't wonder that you call it a diamond.'

'Now let me show you a black diamond,' Hal said, going on to the cage of the black leopard.

'Another prize,' said Ryan. 'It must be very rare.'

'Yes, it is,' Hal agreed. 'Scientists say that there's about one chance in a hundred thousand that a leopard will come out black. But in this next cage we have something that could be one in a million.'

The men could hardly believe their eyes as they studied the double-headed boomslang. The snake, annoyed by their examination, blew up its two neck-balloons to their full size.

'Well I'll be . . .' exclaimed Ryan. 'Never saw anything like it in my life. Does any zoo have a specimen like this?'

'Only one. Two or three other zoos have had two-headed snakes, but they all died young.'

'Why should that be?'

'Because there are two brains, and if one brain tries to go here and the other tries to go there the snake is split apart in the middle.'

'So that's why you put on the collar,' Sims commented. 'For such a young fellow, you seem to know your business very well.'

'Not well enough,' Hal said. 'But I should know it, because as long as I can remember my father has been bringing specimens from all over the world to our animal farm in Long Island. Now come into our bedroom and see our best friends.'

'Don't tell me you have a zoo in your bedroom!'

'Not only in our bedroom, but in our beds. Roger sleeps with two gorillas. I share my bed with a python.'

He took them inside. Instantly a clamour rose from the bush-baby, the elephant shrew, the colobus monkey and the two baby gorillas. Hal introduced the visitors to the adult female gorilla. 'This is Lady Luck – because we were so lucky to get her. Sit down, gentlemen.'

Sims sat on Hal's bed. Something writhed beneath him. He leaped up to find a white head coming out from under the blanket, tongue darting in and out.

'Don't be frightened,' Hal said. 'It's only Snow White.'

The great snake slithered out on the floor. Its blue eyes flashed, its long white body was like a wriggling ray of light.

'Magnificent!' Ryan exclaimed. 'A truly magnificent creature. I never would have thought a snake could be so beautiful. Is it really a python?'

'It is.'

'But isn't it dangerous?'

'No,' Hal said. 'There's no danger between friends.'

As they were leaving, Ryan said, 'You were right. You have a fine collection of diamonds.'

24
A Mystery Solved

That night Roger woke to find one of his bedmates shivering violently.

Bubu, as he had named this small gorilla, was shaking like a leaf in the wind. Yet he was not cold. On the contrary, he seemed much warmer than usual. In fact, he was almost feverish.

Roger woke Hal. 'I think we have a sick baby on our hands.'

Hal tumbled out and lit the oil lamp. He examined Bubu. The little fellow's skin was very hot. Yet he was shaking as if very cold.

'Chills and fever,' Hal said. He felt the pulse. 'Heart is pumping as if he were running uphill.' He put his ear to the ape's chest. 'He seems to have trouble breathing. Little short gasps. Something wrong down in those lungs.'

Roger was impatient. 'Stop fiddling around. Get busy and do something.'

He had confidence in his brother's skill. Generally Hal knew what to do. He could give first aid, treat a case of the flu, sterilize a wound, even perform light surgery.

So Roger was surprised to hear him say, 'I'm afraid this is too serious a thing for me to tinker with. We've got to get this little chap to a hospital.'

'Hospital! Where do you expect to find a hospital in this godforsaken country?'

'There's one on the road to Rutshuru. I don't know whether it's closed or not.'

'Why should it be closed?'

'It was run by white doctors. Most of the white people of the Congo have been killed or have gone home.'

'Then why is it we've had no trouble?'

'No trouble? You forget there've been two attempts to burn down this cabin. And how about that devil, whoever he was, who got me into an elephant pit and pushed in a leopard to kill me? Luckily we're well off the main road and ten thousand feet up the mountain. I wouldn't give two cents for the safety of whites down on the highway. The hospital may be burned down by this time, for all I know. And even if it's still there, the chances are they won't have a veterinarian on their staff.'

'Well, let's go and see.'

The first glimmer of dawn saw them on their way. Hal drove, and Roger held the hot and shivering ape in his arms.

They were relieved to find the hospital still standing.

They rang the bell but there was no answer. They went in. There was no one in the office. There were no nurses bustling about the halls. There were black patients bedded down in the wards – but where were the doctors?

Then in a far ward they found one, bending over a suffering patient.

'Doctor,' Hal said, 'may we speak to you for a moment?'

The man straightened up and looked at them. He was a young fellow, perhaps in his early thirties. His face was haggard, his eyes were sunken pits, he appeared half-starved. He looked as if he had not slept during the past night, perhaps not for many nights.

'Pardon me,' Hal said. 'Is there a veterinarian on your staff?'

'Sorry, no vet. Where's the animal?'

'Right here.'

'But that's no animal,' protested the doctor. Then he corrected himself. 'Of course it is an animal, but not medically speaking. Its anatomy and physiology are like those of a human. It suffers from the same diseases. Let's get this little fellow in bed and see what's the matter with him.'

After his diagnosis, the doctor looked worried. 'Your little friend is seriously ill. Lobar pneumonia. And pleurisy. There's not much chance of saving him. A grown ape may beat off an attack like this, but it's apt to be too much for an infant. We'll do all we can.'

He looked very tired. Hal said, 'You seem to be working alone.'

'Yes. We did have two other doctors. They were both killed. We had five nurses. Two were killed – the other three I sent back to Europe.'

'Then why did you stay on?'

The young doctor refused to say something heroic. He smiled. 'Just stubbornness, I guess. We may have to close after all. It takes money to run a place like this. Funds used to come to us from Europe. Now they no longer get through. What is your friend's name?'

'Friend? Oh, you mean the ape. His name is Bubu.'

'I like to know the name of every one of my patients. They feel better if I can call them by name. Don't worry – I'll do my very best for Bubu.'

Every day they drove down to see Bubu. The little ape was suffering acutely. He was kept awake by chest pain and tortured by a dry, hacking cough. Dr Burton, the young physician, gave him as much attention as any other patient in the hospital.

He kept him on a diet of milk and soup. He used chloral to keep the fever down. One day when the ape was delirious, he had to be quieted with morphine.

Every day Hal and Roger would find him moaning softly, but the moaning would stop when he saw them and he would put out a small hand for Roger to hold.

On the sixth night came the crisis. It was the little ape's last struggle between life and death.

The doctor sat beside his bed all through the night. As morning came, he knew the answer – the ape would live.

His temperature dropped, his pulse slowed, his breathing was less difficult, and instead of being dry and hot, he began to perspire freely.

'Good signs,' said Dr Burton, who was more hollow-eyed and sunken-cheeked than ever, but happy. 'He's coming out of it. A few days more and he'll be on his feet.'

When he was pronounced cured, the boys not only paid the modest sum that the doctor would accept, but made him a present of a carload of food supplies for himself and his patients.

'Especially for you,' Hal said. 'Because if you don't

hold up, what will happen to all your patients?'

'I wish we could really do something for him,' said Roger as they drove home with their convalescent ape. 'Something big.'

'He's having a tough time,' Hal agreed. 'His patients don't pay him anything except a few bananas, he has no funds to keep up the building and buy supplies and pay large enough salaries to persuade doctors and nurses to come down from Europe and take the chance of being massacred. He has a lot of courage to stick it out in spite of all those difficulties.'

The return of Bubu to the bedroom menagerie was welcomed by all of the other members – and Bubu himself crooned with delight as he took his old place in Roger's bed at night.

But it was not to be a night of carefree sleep. Both boys sat bolt upright in bed with popping eyes when the crash of glass told them that the small window had been broken to bits. Hal turned his flashlight on the window and saw that a writhing, twisting, hissing serpentine form was being pushed into the room. It looked very much like the deadly mamba they had captured near the volcano.

Instantly the room was in an uproar. From every

corner came howls, screams, shrieks and whistles, for there was not a creature in the room that did not dread the mamba.

The men also were roused. Hal heard someone – it sounded like Joro – shouting, 'Bring the net.'

Something strange was going on outside. The boys sprang towards the door – then realized that their first job was to take care of the mamba. It was strutting about the room with its head six feet in the air, trying to decide in what creature it should sink its fangs. The rough treatment it had just had and the confinement within four walls, not to mention the rushing about of all the terrified inmates, were enough to increase its usual bad temper.

Hal got his revolver. Roger yelled, 'No – a sack.'

A sack over a snake's head was usually enough to quiet it.

'We have no sack,' Hal said.

He prepared to shoot – making sure that there was no animal beyond the snake in line with its head.

'Wait a minute,' Roger cried, and ripped the blanket from his bed. He faced the snake, whose head was a foot above his own. The mamba lunged, with the evident intention of sinking its fangs in his face. But

Roger was too quick for it. He flung the blanket, and the poison-squirting teeth spilled their venom in the thick cloth. He brought the blanket down over the snake's head.

Hal was right there with a length of rope which he flung round the blanket just below the head and tied it tight. The mamba dropped to the floor and lay still.

'We'll take care of it later,' Hal said. 'Let's see what's going on.'

Outside they found the men trying to get the heavy net over a dark monster about the size of Tieg. But it was not Tieg. Hal's flashlight revealed the features of a huge gorilla. Roger recognized him.

'It's Gog!'

There is no gentler ape than the gorilla – yet Gog's face, at this moment, was distorted with anger and agony. Now he was ninety-nine per cent killer.

He overtopped all these petty humans and he had the strength of any ten of them. He tried to clutch them with his long arms as big around as a ship's boom with fingers the size of Coca-Cola bottles.

The men got the net over him. It was made of heavy green vine, stronger than rope, but he tore holes in it. He

tossed the men around like paper dolls. He shrieked like a maddened elephant.

Plainly, someone – perhaps more than one – would be killed. The net wasn't enough. Hal plunged into the cabin and came out with the dart gun. He fired. The dart embedded itself in the upper arm and the tranquillizing M99 flowed into the gorilla's system.

It was enough to put a zebra to sleep. But not enough for the giant Gog. Hal ran to get another dart of the same strength, and delivered its contents into the other arm.

The infuriated beast completed the job of tearing the net to bits. Now his arms were free. He thrust them both forward, seized two men and knocked their heads together. He swept both arms backwards, mowing down men on both sides as if they were ninepins in a bowling alley. From tip to tip those arms had a reach of a good eight feet – so that the fantastic creature was actually a foot broader than he was tall.

The men who were still standing lost no time in getting out of the way of those deadly arms. One of those terrific twelve-pound hams could kill a man.

Since no one was within reach at the moment, the ape vented his fury by screaming and slapping his chest. What a barrel of a chest it was, five feet round. He drew in his breath to inflate it as much as possible. The pounding of this great air-filled tank produced a sound like the beating of a huge African drum.

It was his last act of defiance. His arms dropped to his sides, his eyes closed, and he fell in a heap.

'Quick!' Hal exclaimed. 'The rhino car.'

The Powerwagon was backed up to within a couple of feet of the prostrate giant. It was equipped with a cage large enough and strong enough so that even the most furious rhino could not break his way out of it.

'Lay hold!' Hal ordered.

How do you take hold of a gorilla? Everything about him was too large to provide a convenient handhold. It took a deal of puffing, straining and grunting before the men succeeded in hoisting the seven-hundred-pound monster into the cage.

'Don't close the gate,' Hal said.

He climbed into the cage, knelt beside the ape, and ran his hand through the long matted hair.

'Here it is,' he said at last. 'The place where the bullet got him.'

Now everything was clear. This really was Gog. Somehow he had broken into the mamba's cage and had put the snake into the boys' room with intent to kill. He must have been the one who had thrown the leopard into the pit with Hal, and had twice tried to burn down the cabin. All because of love for his family and the pain of a festering wound.

Hal drew out his fingers. They were covered with green pus. 'Poor devil,' Hal said. 'Worse than I thought.'

'Can you treat it?' Roger asked.

'I'm afraid it's beyond me. The bullet is lodged in the shoulder joint. I might have gotten it out if we could have nabbed him just after he was shot. But by this time it has set up a very bad infection. I've never seen a worse abscess. And the bullet must be wedged in between the humerus and the scapula where it must grind every time the arm is moved. I'd hate to think how painful it must be. No wonder he's turned rogue. I won't tinker with it – this is another job for Dr Burton.'

25
The Inquisitive Ostrich

When Gog was laid on a hospital bed, it promptly collapsed under the seven-hundred pound patient.

'No matter,' the doctor said. 'If he won't stay up, he'll just have to stay down. We haven't anything strong enough to hold him. First of all I think I'd better give him an anaesthetic to keep him asleep while I'm digging for that bullet.'

Roger was shaking his head. 'If he's asleep, he won't know.'

'Won't know what?' Hal said.

'Won't know we're trying to help him.'

The doctor looked surprised. 'Why is that so important?'

Roger explained. 'He thinks we killed his family. And the man who was with us put that bullet into him. It's made a rogue out of him. He just has no use for the human race. He's one great big hate.'

The doctor looked at Hal. Hal said, 'I think perhaps my brother has something there. The way this gorilla feels now he's too dangerous to be put on exhibit in any animal collection. He's quite likely to murder somebody. In fact he tried to murder us last night. Stuffed a mamba in through the window. And twice he's tried to burn us out. And thanks to him I had to fight a leopard in an elephant pit. Those things were a mystery to us, but now we know he was the guilty one.'

'You two are pretty amazing,' the doctor remarked. 'I think if I were in your shoes I would just put another bullet into this rascal and finish him off for good and all.'

Hal smiled. 'Killing animals doesn't happen to be our business. We take them alive, tame them and send them home for other people to enjoy. And there's nothing that tames an animal so quickly as the knowledge that you're trying to do it a good turn.'

'But do you think this animal is intelligent enough to realize that I'm trying to do him a good turn when he wakes and finds me digging into his shoulder?'

Hal nodded. 'I think any animal that's intelligent enough to plan murder the way he planned it is bright enough to know when he's being helped. But perhaps you'd rather not risk it.'

'I'll risk it,' said Dr Burton. 'But first I'll get these three other patients out of here.'

The three men were transferred to another room. Then the door was locked and the doctor went to work.

The probing in the wound woke the gorilla. Gog slowly opened his eyes. He growled when he saw his two mortal enemies. He was still too sleepy to do more. Hal was bending over him and Roger was sitting on the floor holding the ape's hands as if he were a baby to be comforted instead of a giant who could kill the boy with one slap. And someone was easing that painful thing out of his shoulder.

It came away at last in the grip of the forceps and the doctor held it before the eyes of the ape. Gog looked searchingly into the faces of the three men. There was no growling now. He winced a little when the doctor proceeded to clean out the abscess but he bore the treatment patiently.

Then came the dressing – it soothed the inflamed nerves. What a blessed relief!

When Gog closed his eyes Roger began to remove his hand, but the ape held onto it. Only after he was sound asleep was Roger able to withdraw his hand and join Hal and the doctor in the corridor.

'Well,' the doctor said, 'I've just seen a miracle. You

certainly seem to know what makes an animal tick.'

'The same thing that makes a human animal tick,' Hal said. 'Gorillas respond quickly to good treatment. But don't take it for granted that Gog has suddenly turned from a devil into an angel. That would be expecting a little too much.'

'Don't worry,' Burton said. 'I won't take any unnecessary chances. No other patients will be put back in that room. Your Mr Gog shall have the distinction of being the only patient in the hospital to have a private room.'

'How long will he need to be here?'

'Just until tomorrow. Then you can continue the treatment at home.

Joro came running down the hall. 'Bwana. Come quick. Ostrich.'

Sure enough, and a very handsome one it was, strutting across the hospital grounds.

Hal had wanted to add an ostrich to his collection. But perhaps this one was a pet.

'Is it yours?' he asked Dr Burton.

'No, no. Just a wild bird. But we see it often. It wanders around here and in the nearby villages picking up whatever it can find.'

'You mean scraps of food.'

'Not only food, but hard objects, stones, rings that it pulls off the ears of the women, anything bright and shiny. It will steal anything from anybody. But it belongs to nobody. You are free to take it if you want it.'

Hal went into action. Luckily he had most of his crew with him, since they had come along to carry Gog into the hospital. He instructed them to make a circle round the ostrich. Then they could gradually close in on it and capture it.

He and Roger came close to the bird to study its plumage and decide whether it would make a good specimen.

The ostrich made no attempt to run off. Instead, it examined the boys curiously, then began to pluck at their clothing. Roger put up his hand to fend off the inquisitive beak.

Quick as a flash, the ostrich plucked the watch from his wrist and swallowed it.

'My watch,' cried Roger. 'How am I going to get that back? What does it want with these hard things anyhow?'

'The ostrich has no teeth,' Hal said. 'So it can't chew its food. The gravel and other hard objects it swallows do the chewing. They churn around in the stomach and grind up the food.'

'Look,' Roger said. 'Now it's eating stones. See it making for that flashy one. What kind of a stone is that?'

Hal had only an instant to study the stone before it was swallowed. Reflecting the sun, it shone like a jewel. It was as if there were a light inside it. He suddenly remembered that the geologist Ryan had described a diamond just that way. He searched the ground but didn't find another like it. But wasn't it important to learn whether it really was a diamond?

'We've got to get inside that bird,' he said. 'Toto, bring the dart gun.'

The tranquillizer worked fast. As soon as the bird closed its eyes and sank to the ground, Hal directed the men to take it up and tote it into the hospital.

When Dr Burton saw his new patient he protested. 'You must think I'm running a Noah's Ark,' he laughed.

'If I'm not mistaken,' Hal said, 'there's something in this bird more valuable than all the contents of the Ark put together.' He told of what he had seen. 'Do you think you can get at it?'

'A fairly simple operation,' the doctor said. 'Just a slit

to open the stomach, take out what's inside, and sew it up again.'

Skilfully, he proceeded to do just that. One of the first things to emerge was Roger's watch, still ticking away merrily. Out came half-digested lucerne, lettuce, grass and wild celery, mixed with an odd assortment of grinders, gravel, buttons, keys, spoons, and even a set of false teeth lost a few days before by a village headman.

And the bright stone.

Dr Burton examined it with interest. 'I'm no expert on diamonds. We could send this to town to be assayed.'

'We can do better than that,' Hal said. He told the doctor about the visit of the Williamson geologists. 'They said they'd be in Rutshuru today. We can go over right now and try to locate them.'

The ostrich, relieved of twelve pounds of gravel and trinkets, was placed in the cage that had housed Gog and taken home to join the mountain menagerie. Most of the men went along, while Hal and Roger drove to Rutshuru. They found the geologists in the town's one small hotel. They examined the luminous bit of rock and pronounced it a diamond.

'It's the real thing,' Ryan exclaimed. 'Can you take us where you found this?'

Within half an hour they were poking around with shovels in the plot of ground where the diamond had been discovered. A few feet under the wind-blown dust, they found what they were looking for – the surface of a diamond lode that might extend downwards, funnel-shaped, for hundreds or even thousands of feet.

'You have struck it rich,' they told the boys. 'We'll ask you to sign preliminary papers. Then we'll bring in some of our men and do some actual digging. When we get a better idea of the extent of the lode our firm will make an advance payment to you and a royalty arrangement.'

'That's fine,' Hal said, 'except that you're making one mistake. This is on the hospital grounds. Your arrangements will be made with Dr Burton, not with us.'

Ryan looked surprised. 'But you located the deposit. You're entitled to a share of the profits.'

'Listen,' Hal said. 'This hospital is doing a grand job under terrible difficulties. The hospital is about to close down for lack of funds. The people need this hospital. They even come from a hundred miles away. Dr Burton is frightfully overworked. He's doing it all alone. His doctors and nurses have been killed or have gone home. He needs money to recruit new staff, buy supplies, instruments, new equipment – and here it all is, right in his own front yard.'

'But your father – isn't he the boss? Don't you want to cable him for instructions?'

'We know exactly what Father would say. We're animal collectors, not miners.'

The geologists shook their heads over the stubbornness of two young men, and went in to see Dr Burton.

25
Shipload of Rascals

The freighter, *African Star*, had thirty-four passengers. But only twelve of them were human. The other twenty-two were listed on the ship's manifest as follows:

'One gorilla, male; 1 gorilla, female; 2 infant gorillas; 1 python, white; 1 elephant shrew; 1 colobus monkey; 1 kudu; 1 bush-baby; 1 chimpanzee; 1 sitatunga; 1 mamba; 1 spitting cobra; 1 boomslang; 1 black leopard; 3 vervet monkeys; 1 ostrich; 1 Gaboon viper; 2 skunks.'

The viper and the skunks had been added at the last moment. The captain had objected to the skunks, even though Hal assured him that they were a very rare variety. That didn't improve their smell.

The captain consented only after Hal sprayed them with perfume and promised to keep them sprayed during the voyage.

This was the most important wildlife shipment to leave Mombasa in many a day. Hal and Roger had decided to go along to see that the animals were properly fed and cared for. They had another reason. They were a bit homesick.

'And we ought to be on hand in case of accidents,' Hal said.

Roger asked, 'What accidents?'

'Accidents can happen,' said Hal.

At first everything went smoothly. For five days the ship sailed over tranquil seas down the coast past Dar-es-Salaam, Durban and Capetown.

Rounding the Cape, she ran into rough weather and began to roll. The animals in their boxes and cages on the deck amidships started to fret. They were not used to any such motion. Some became seasick. All began to use whatever voice Nature had given them. The muttering and moaning grew into a screaming chorus.

This touched the heart of the chimp, Good Samaritan. Sam was such a close friend of man that he had not been caged. He had gone about with Hal and Roger daily as they opened each container just enough to put in food. For simplicity's sake, all locks took the same key. It was kept handy in a box nailed to the kudu's cage.

Now Sam saw his opportunity to do a good deed. He began with the little colobus monkey he had befriended on the slope of the volcano. The poor little fellow was wailing pitifully, pulling at the bars, trying to escape from his teetering box.

The angel of mercy came to his aid. Sam got the key and unlocked the door. Out tumbled 'The Little Bishop'. His wailing stopped. Happily he dashed about the deck, his white robe floating behind him.

Then he joyously clambered into the rigging and took a flying leap to the ladder that scaled the mast. It was as good as a tree. Here he did not mind the motion. Trees also sway in a storm.

Quite pleased with the results of his charitable deed, Helpful Harry opened another box. Out slithered the mamba. At once it reared six feet high. Ungratefully, it lunged at the chimp, who dodged just in time.

Sam was a bit disappointed. He considered this a poor way for the twisty creature to say thanks. Oh well, you couldn't expect appreciation from everybody.

The mamba slipped on the sloping deck and skidded down a companionway to the passenger deck. Irritated by being so tossed about, it looked for someone to punish. Anyone would do.

Rounding a corner, the snake came face to face with a passenger, a lady from Pocatello, Idaho. Needless to say, this was a shock to the good lady, since snakes six feet tall are not commonly encountered on the streets of Pocatello.

The mamba made a pass at her. Its fangs dug into

empty air, for madam had already collapsed in a quivering faint on the deck.

The snake contemptuously walked over her. Discovering a partly open door, it entered. It was disappointed to find no enemy.

But there was a place to hide. The absent passenger, member of a fireman's band, had left his tuba standing against the wall.

It was a double bass, largest of all brass instruments, ideal retreat for a badly disturbed snake. Gratefully, it wound its way down into the dark interior.

In the meantime Sam the chimp had opened a dozen more doors. The black leopard turned white. Biting everything it found, it crunched a tap and let out a cascade of water that fell into a pail of detergent. Suds frothed all over the deck and over the big cat. The slippery animal skidded from one bulwark to the other at every roll of the ship.

The three vervet monkeys, wildly delighted to be free, scampered up the rigging, leaped from boom to boom, and got themselves liberally pasted by the fresh white paint the crew had been applying to the ship for arrival at her home port.

Then the monkeys took a notion to explore below.

They tumbled into the coal hole and came up black with coal dust which they liberally applied to the freshly painted funnels, rails and bulkheads until the ship looked like a zebra in its coat of black stripes on white.

Colliding with the supercargo, they gave his white tropicals a thorough dusting and his bare arms a few good bites as he tried in vain to capture them and restore them to their box.

He gave up, and went to beat on the door of the cabin occupied by the animal collectors. These two carefree gentlemen were having a pleasant siesta after spending much of the night on watch over their uneasy charges.

'Come alive,' he yelled. 'Your beasts are tearing up the ship. Wake up, you blokes.'

Hal, recognizing the voice of the supercargo, replied sleepily, 'Can't you watch them while we get a bit of sleep? The animals are cargo, aren't they? And aren't you in charge of cargo?'

The supercargo fairly screamed, 'I tell you, they're all over the ship.'

More convincing than the excitement of the officer was what Hal saw when he opened his eyes. The spitting cobra was looking in the window. It seemed ready to spit, and Hal was directly in its line of fire.

Hal's immediate thought was of the passengers. This creature, on the loose, could blind and even kill. The best thing that could be done was to get it to spit, and spit now, so its venom would be exhausted before it endangered anyone else.

But even he didn't particularly care to be its victim. There was a mirror at the end of the cabin facing the window. Thinking fast, he leaped out of his bunk into a corner by the door.

Now the snake could not see him – but could see his reflection in the mirror. Hal grabbed a flashlight and played it on his face. The brightly lit image in the mirror was all the cobra needed.

It let loose its load of venom, which travelled like a bullet over the ten feet between the window and the provocative eyes. The glass streamed with the white poison.

Hal moved to catch the snake, but it had already gone. But now it was almost as harmless as a garter snake.

The boys plunged out on deck and caught whatever they could lay their hands on. But they couldn't be everywhere at once. The whole ship was in an uproar – passengers screaming, alarm bells ringing, animals squawking, chattering, whistling, shrieking.

The tuba player, returning to his cabin, thought to add to the alarm by blowing a blast on his instrument. He gave it all his lung-power, but there was no sound. Instead, the blazing eyes and darting tongue of a disturbed mamba appeared over the tuba's rim. The musician left the tuba to the snake and dived out on deck.

The ostrich, with its peculiar ability to roar like a lion and kick like a mule, was engaging in battle with the supercargo. The man naturally considered himself able to conquer any bird, even the eight-foot giant. He would just jump on it and flatten it to the deck.

But when he tried this manoeuvre it didn't work. The three-hundred-pound bird just didn't flatten. Instead, the hundred-and-sixty-pound supercargo found himself riding ostrich-back clutching feathers to keep from falling.

Passing the canvas swimming pool, the bird veered sharply and over went the unlucky rider with his hands full of feathers. Into the pool he fell, and came up to see the ostrich dart its head in through a cabin window, pluck a safety razor from a passenger in mid-shave and swallow it – then dash on with its beak dripping great gobs of shaving cream.

The skunks scampered into the lounge where several

passengers had taken refuge. The steward succeeded in catching them both by the tail; whereupon they let loose their barrage of scent, quite different from the perfume that had graced their fur, and choking passengers fled to the deck.

The python, Snow White, emerged when her door was opened, but quickly tired of the wild commotion. Very sensibly she retired into a cabin and, seeing a bed, slipped into it, snuggling up gratefully against the lady who already occupied it. She, with her eyes screwed shut, was too paralysed to realize that her blankets were being shared by another lady more distinguished than herself.

The Good Samaritan, having completed his good deed, thought it was time to have a little fun himself.

He made for the bridge, tumbled into the wheel-house, and so startled the helmsman that he fled, shouting for the captain.

The chimp took the wheel. He had often watched what went on in this high spot. He knew just what to do. He first blew a lusty blast on the whistle. Then he seized a handle and signalled the engineer – full speed ahead, full speed reverse, and every point between, until the sweating men in the engine room were convinced that the helmsman of the *African Star* had gone stark, staring mad.

Only the great Gog kept his head. He went about with Hal and Roger seizing animals and restoring them to their cages.

When Roger attempted to extract the mamba from the tuba, the snake struck out at his chest – but before it could get there a great arm barred its way and the fangs went deep into the flesh of the ape.

Roger at once cut the wound and put his mouth to the arm to suck out the poison. Then Hal promptly injected the life-saving serum.

Hal said, 'When you consider that apes have a deadly fear of snakes, that was a brave thing your hairy friend did. And to think that a week ago he would very cheerfully have killed you himself. It just shows – something.'

25
Diving Adventure

It was good to be home. Good to see their mother and father. Good to look across the broad acres of the Hunt wild-animal farm, alive with animals from all over the world awaiting transfer to zoos, circuses and scientific institutions.

'And some of the finest are the ones you have just brought home,' John Hunt said. 'I asked you to get a big male gorilla. But I never expected one seven feet tall. I asked for a python, any python, and you get one in a million, a pure-white blue-eyed beauty. And a two-headed boomslang that is a scientific marvel. And that beautiful colobus, and the six-foot-tall mamba. And not just a leopard, but the rare black leopard. And all the things I didn't ask for. I'm proud of you both – because you have the right idea: to do more than you are asked to do.'

'Seems to me,' Hal said, 'you've been doing the same thing. That sign over your gate.'

When they left home, the sign had read:

JOHN HUNT
WILDLIFE

Now it read:

JOHN HUNT AND SONS
WILDLIFE

'You didn't need to do that,' Hal said.

'Only fair,' said his father, and dismissed the subject.

He set down the bush-baby and the elephant shrew, which he had been holding in his lap, and took up the two skunks. He admired their great bushy tails.

'Like bird-of-paradise plumes,' he said.

Whether or not the skunks understood the compliment, they understood the man. He had 'a way with animals' – a magic that he had passed on to his sons. Skunks are charming pets, if they will just hold their fire. These felt safe with the animal man, therefore he was safe from them.

'Well, boys, perhaps you'll stay home now and take a good rest.'

The boys' faces fell a foot. Rest is about the last thing a boy wants.

'I have another project,' John Hunt said. 'But someone else can handle it.'

'What's the project?' Roger asked breathlessly.

'Don't tell them, John,' said Mrs Hunt. 'It's too dangerous. I'd worry all the time.'

'No harm in telling them,' John said. 'They're members of the firm. They'll have to know sooner or later.'

Hal grew impatient. 'Get on with it, Dad. What've you got up your sleeve?'

'I have oceanography up my sleeve. I'm sure you know what that is.'

'Exploring beneath the sea,' Hal said.

'Right. And you know how important it is. Practically all of the world's land surface has been explored. But less than five per cent of the ocean bottom. We know more about the back side of the moon, two hundred and forty thousand miles away, than about the waters at our front door. Of course we should learn about the moon – but as our astronaut, Scott Carpenter, has said, "Deep-sea research will pay off in richer rewards much sooner."'

'He should know,' Hal said. 'He's the only one who has been both up and down.'

'Yes. After his space flight, he lived thirty days in a home beneath the sea. That's where the treasures are – treasures we need, now that the land can't produce enough meat, milk, fish, vegetables, all sorts of food, oil, gas, gold, silver, aluminium, manganese and the thousand other things necessary to keep life going on this planet. They are all down there, at the bottom of the sea. This year, another home has been built for undersea explorers.'

'Where is it?' Hal asked.

'In one of the most exciting seas in the world. Near Australia, just off the Great Barrier Reef.'

Roger came alive. He had read thrilling stories of the dangerous waters and swarming sea life along the Great Barrier Reef, longest coral reef in the world.

'Could we get in on this deal?' he asked eagerly.

'You're invited,' John Hunt said. 'They know about your underwater work in the Pacific. One of the scientists they need is a naturalist. He must be young, strong and experienced. They think Hal would fill the bill.'

Hal was elated. Roger was gloomy.

'But how about me?' Roger said.

'They also need an errand boy.'

'Errand boy! You're kidding. An errand boy at the bottom of the sea?'

'Exactly. You would have your own diving saucer. You would run errands – carrying up specimens to the surface ship, bringing down supplies. And helping your brother catch deep-sea creatures, large and small, that are needed for study in aquariums and laboratories.'

'My own diving saucer,' Roger chuckled.

'Don't think it will be just a big game,' his father warned. 'Plenty of hard work. And danger. The sharks along that reef are the world's worst. Australia reports more killings by sharks than all other countries put together. Think about it seriously.'

And the outcome of the more or less serious thought that the boys devoted to this proposal will be recounted in the next book, *Diving Adventure*.

AMAZON ADVENTURE

'No one has ever come out alive.'

Hal and Roger Hunt crash-land into the middle of a pioneering expedition to the unmapped regions of the greatest jungle on earth: the Amazon. And when their mission to explore the uncharted territory of the Pastaza River goes off course . . . it's the survival of the fittest.

ARCTIC ADVENTURE

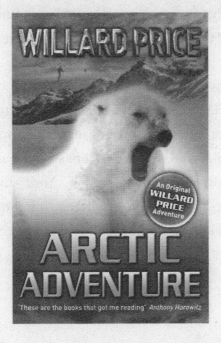

'Adrift in a savage land of ice and snow . . .'

Hal and Roger Hunt are colder than they've ever been in their lives, up among the ice floes of Greenland. This harsh land holds many dangers, from killer whales to grizzly bears, but an evil man may turn out to be the deadliest threat the boys have to face.

WILLARD PRICE

Willard Price was born in 1887 in Peterborough, Ontario. He had a special interest in natural history, ethnology and exploration and made numerous expeditions for the American Museum of Natural History and the National Geographic Society.

He went on to edit various magazines on travel and world affairs and spent six years working in Japan as foreign correspondent for New York and London newspapers. He wrote fourteen adventure stories featuring Hal and Roger Hunt. He died in 1983.